P9-DZP-166

A Bit on the Side

By the Same Author

NOVELS
The Old Boys
The Boarding House
The Love Department
Mrs Eckdorf in O'Neill's Hotel
Miss Gomez and the Brethren
Elizabeth Alone
The Children of Dynmouth
Other People's Worlds
Fools of Fortune
The Silence in the Garden
Felicia's Journey
Death in Summer
The Story of Lucy Gault

NOVELLAS
Nights at Alexandra
Two Lives

SHORT STORIES
The Day We Got Drunk on Cake
The Ballroom of Romance
Angels at the Ritz
Lovers of Their Time
Beyond the Pale
The News from Ireland
Family Sins
The Collected Stories
After Rain
The Hill Bachelors

PLAY
Scenes from an Album

NON-FICTION
A Writer's Ireland
Excursions in the Real World

FOR CHILDREN
Juliet's Story

A Bit on the Side

WILLIAM TREVOR

VIKING

VIKING
Published by the Penguin Group
Penguin Group (USA) Inc., 375 Hudson Street, New York, New York 10014, U.S.A.
Penguin Group (Canada), 10 Alcorn Avenue, Toronto, Ontario, Canada M4V 3B2
(a division of Pearson Penguin Canada Inc.)
Penguin Books Ltd, 80 Strand, London WC2R 0RL, England
Penguin Ireland, 25 St. Stephen's Green, Dublin 2, Ireland (a division of Penguin Books Ltd)
Penguin Group (Australia), 250 Camberwell Road, Camberwell,
Victoria 3124, Australia (a division of Pearson Australia Group Pty Ltd)
Penguin Books India Pvt Ltd, 11 Community Centre, Panchsheel Park,
New Delhi – 110 017, India
Penguin Group (NZ), Cnr Airborne and Rosedale Roads, Albany, Auckland, New Zealand
(a division of Pearson New Zealand Ltd)
Penguin Books (South Africa) (Pty) Ltd, 24 Sturdee Avenue,
Rosebank, Johannesburg 2196, South Africa

Penguin Books Ltd, Registered Offices: 80 Strand, London WC2R 0RL, England

First American edition
Published in 2004 by Viking Penguin,
a member of Penguin Group (USA) Inc.

10 9 8 7 6 5 4 3 2 1

Copyright © William Trevor, 2004
All rights reserved

"Sitting with the Dead," "Traditions," "Justina's Priest," "Sacred Statues," "Big Bucks," "On the Streets," and "A Bit on the Side" first appeared in *The New Yorker;* "Graillis's Legacy" in *New Statesman;* "Solitude" in *Glimmer Train;* and "Rose Wept" in *The Spectator* and *Harper's.*

Publisher's Note
These selections are works of fiction. Names, characters, places, and incidents either are the product of the author's imagination or are used fictitiously, and any resemblance to actual persons, living or dead, business establishments, events, or locales is entirely coincidental.

Library of Congress Cataloging-in-Publication Data

Trevor, William
  A bit on the side / William Trevor.
  p.   cm.
  Contents: Sitting with the dead—Traditions—Justina's priest—An evening out—
Graillis's legacy—Solitude—Sacred statues—Rose wept—Big bucks—On the streets—
The dancing-master's music—A bit on the side.
  ISBN 0-670-03343-X
  I. Title.
PR6070.R4B57 2004
823'.91—dc22   2004042035

This book is printed on acid-free paper. ♾

Printed in the United States of America

Without limiting the rights under copyright reserved above, no part of this publication may be reproduced, stored in or introduced into a retrieval system, or transmitted, in any form or by any means (electronic, mechanical, photocopying, recording or otherwise), without the prior written permission of both the copyright owner and the above publisher of this book.

The scanning, uploading, and distribution of this book via the Internet or via any other means without the permission of the publisher is illegal and punishable by law. Please purchase only authorized electronic editions and do not participate in or encourage electronic piracy of copyrightable materials. Your support of the author's rights is appreciated.

Contents

A Bit on the Side

Sitting with the Dead

His eyes had been closed and he opened them, saying he wanted to see the stable-yard.

Emily's expression was empty of response. Her face, younger than his and yet not seeming so, was empty of everything except the tiredness she felt. 'From the window?' she said.

No, he'd go down, he said. 'Will you get me the coat? And have the boots by the door.'

She turned away from the bed. He would manage on his own if she didn't help him: she'd known him for twenty-eight years, been married to him for twenty-three. Whether or not she brought the coat up to him would make no difference, any more than it would if she protested.

'It could kill you,' she said.

'The fresh air'd strengthen a man.'

Downstairs, she placed the boots ready for him at the back door. She brought his cap and muffler to him with his overcoat. A stitch was needed where the left sleeve met the shoulder, she noticed. She hadn't before and knew he wouldn't wait while she repaired it now.

'What're you going to do there?' she asked, and he said nothing much. Tidy up a bit, he said.

*

He died eight days later, and Dr Ann explained that tidying the stable-yard with only a coat over his pyjamas wouldn't have hastened anything. An hour after she left, the Geraghtys came to the house, not knowing that he was dead.

It was half past seven in the evening then. At the same time the next morning, Keane the undertaker was due. She said that to the Geraghtys, making sure they understood, not wanting them to think she was turning them away for some other reason. Although she knew that if her husband had been alive he wouldn't have agreed to have the Geraghtys at his bedside. It was a relief that they had come too late.

The Geraghtys were two middle-aged women, sisters, the Misses Geraghty, who sat with the dying. Emily had heard of them, but did not know them, not even to see: they'd had to give their name when she opened the door to them. It had never occurred to her that the Geraghtys would attempt to bring their good works to the sick-room she had lived with herself for the last seven months. They were Legion of Mary women, famed for their charity, tireless in their support of the Society of St Vincent de Paul and their promulgation of the writings of Father Xavier O'Shea, a local priest who, at a young age in the 1880s, had contracted malaria in the mission fields of the East.

'We only heard of your trouble Tuesday,' the thinner and smaller of the two apologized. 'It does happen the occasional time we wouldn't hear.'

The other woman, more robust and older, allowed herself jewellery and make-up and took more care with her clothes. But it was her quiet, sharp-featured sister who took the lead.

'We heard in MacClincy's,' she said.

'I'm sorry you've had a wasted journey.'

'It's never wasted.' There was a pause, as if a pause was necessary here. 'You have our sympathy,' was added to that, the explanation of why the journey had not been in vain.

The conversation took place entirely at the hall door. Dusk was becoming dark, but over the white-washed wall of the small front garden Emily still could see a car drawn up in the road. It was cold, the wind gone round to the east. They meant well, these women, even if they'd got everything wrong, driving out from Carra to visit a man who wouldn't have welcomed them and then arriving too late, a man whose death had spared them an embarrassment.

'Would you like a cup of tea?' Emily offered.

She imagined they'd refuse and then begin to go, saying they couldn't disturb her at a time like this. But the big, wide-shouldered one glanced at her sister, hesitating.

'If you're alone,' the smaller one said, 'you'd be welcome to our company. If it would be of help to you.'

*

The dead man had been without religion. Anyone could have told them that, Emily reflected, making tea. He would have said that there was more to their sitting at the bedsides of the ill than met the eye, and she wondered if that could possibly be so. Did they in their compassionate travels hope for the first signs of the belief that often came out of nowhere when death declared its intention? Did they drive away from the houses they visited, straight to a presbytery, their duty done? She had never heard that said about the Geraghtys and she didn't want to believe it. They meant well, she said to herself again.

When they left, she wouldn't go back upstairs to look at the dead features. She'd leave him now to Keane in the morning. In the brief time that had elapsed a day had been settled for the funeral, Thursday of next week; in the morning she would let a few people know; she'd put a notice in the *Advertiser*. No children had been born: when Thursday had passed everything would be over except for the unpaid debts. She buttered slices of brack and stirred the tea in the pot. She carried in the tray.

They hadn't taken their coats off, but sat as still as statues, a little apart from one another.

'It's cold,' she said, 'I'll light the fire.'

'Ah no. Ah no, don't bother.' They both protested, but she did anyway, and the kindling that had been in the grate all summer flared up at once. She poured their tea, asking if they took sugar, and then offering the brack. They began to call her Emily, as if they knew her well. They gave their own names: Kathleen the older sister, and Norah.

'I didn't think,' Kathleen began to say, and Norah interrupted her.

'Oh, we know all right,' she said. 'You're Protestant here, but that never made a difference yet.'

They had sat with the Methodist minister, the Reverend Wolfe, Kathleen said. They'd read to him, they'd brought in whatever he wanted. They were there when he went.

'Never a difference,' Norah repeated, and in turn they took a slice of brack. They commented on it, saying it was excellent.

'It isn't easy,' Kathleen said when the conversation lapsed. 'The first few hours. We often stay.'

'It was good of you to think of him.'

'It's cheerful with that fire, Emily,' Kathleen said.

They asked her about the horses because the horses were what they'd heard about, and she explained that they'd become a thing of the past. She'd sell the place now, she said.

'You'd find it remote, Emily,' Kathleen said. Her lipstick had left a trace on the rim of the teacup and

Norah drew her attention to it with a gesture. Kathleen wiped it off. 'We're town people ourselves,' she said.

Emily didn't consider the house she'd lived in for nearly thirty years remote. Five minutes in the car and you were in the middle of Carra. Mangan's Bridge, in the other direction, was no more than a minute.

'You get used to a place,' Emily said.

They identified for her the house where they lived themselves, on the outskirts of Carra, on the Athy road. Emily knew it, a pleasant creeper-covered house with silver railings in front of it, not big but prosperous-looking. She'd thought it was Corrigan's, the surveyor's.

'I don't know why I thought that.'

'We bought it from Mr Corrigan,' Norah said, 'when we came to Carra three years ago.' And her sister said they'd been living in Athy before that.

'Carra was what we were looking for,' Norah said.

They were endeavouring to lift her spirits, Emily realized, by keeping things light. Carra had improved in their time, they said, and it would again. You could tell with a town; some of them wouldn't rise out of the doldrums while a century'd go by.

'You'd maybe come in to Carra now?' Kathleen said.

'I don't know what I'll do.'

She poured more tea. She handed round the brack again. Dr Ann had given her pills to take, but she didn't intend to take them. Exhausted as she was, she didn't want to sleep.

'He went out a week ago,' she said. 'He got up and went out to the yard with only a coat over his pyjamas. I thought it was that that hurried it on, but seemingly it wasn't.'

They didn't say anything, just nodded, both of them. She said he had been seven months dying. He hadn't read a newspaper all that time, she said. In the end all the food he could manage was cornflour.

'We never knew your husband,' Norah said, 'any more than yourself. Although I think we maybe met him on the road one day.'

A feeling of apprehension began in Emily, a familiar dread that compulsively caused one hand to clench the other, fingers tightly locking. People often met him, exercising one of the horses. A car would slow down for him but he never acknowledged it, never so much as raised the crop. For a moment she forget that he was dead.

'He was often out,' she said.

'Oh, this was long ago.'

'He sold the last of the horses twelve months ago. He didn't want them left.'

'He raced his horses, we're to understand?' Kathleen said.

'Point-to-points. Punchestown the odd time.'

'Well, that's great.'

'There wasn't much success.'

'It's an up and down business, of course.'

Disappointment had filled the house when yet again

a horse trailed in, when months of preparation went for nothing. There had never been much reason for optimism, but even so expectation had been high, as if anything less would have brought bad luck. When Emily married, her husband had been training a string of yearlings on the Curragh. Doing well, he'd said himself, although in fact he wasn't.

'You never had children, Emily?' Kathleen asked.

'No, we never did.'

'I think we heard that said.'

The house had been left to her by an aunt on her mother's side. Forty-three acres, sheep kept; and the furniture had been left to her too. 'I used come here as a child. A Miss Edgill my aunt was. Did you hear of her?'

They shook their heads. Way before their time, Kathleen said, looking around her. A good house, she said.

'She'd no one else to leave it to.' And Emily didn't add that neither the property nor the land would ever have become hers if her aunt had suspected she'd marry the man she had.

'You'll let it go though?' Kathleen pursued her enquiries, doing her best to knit together a conversation. 'The way things are now, you were saying you'd let it go?'

'I don't know.'

'Anyone would require a bit of time.'

'We see a lot of widowing,' Norah murmured.

'Nearly to the day, we were married twenty-three years.'

'God took him because He wanted him, Emily.'

The Geraghtys continued to offer sympathy, one following the other in what was said, the difference in tone and manner continuing also. And again – and more often as more solace was pressed upon her – Emily reflected how fortunate it was that they had escaped the awkwardness of attempting to keep company with her husband. He would have called her back as soon as she'd left them with him. He would have asked her who they were, although he knew; he would have told her to take them away. He'd never minded what he said – the flow of coarse language when someone crossed one of the fields, every word shouted out, frighteningly sometimes. It was always that: raising his voice, the expressions he used; not once, not ever, had there been violence. Yet often she had wished that there had been, believing that violence would have been easier to bear than the power of his articulated anger. It was power she had always felt coming from him, festering and then released, his denial of his failure.

'The horses. Punchestown. The world of the racecourse,' Kathleen said. 'You've had an interesting life, Emily.'

It seemed to Emily that Norah was about to shake her head, that for the first time the sisters were on the verge of a disagreement. It didn't surprise her: the observation that had been made astonished her.

'Unusual is what my sister means.' Norah nodded her correction into place, her tone softening the contradiction.

'There's many a woman doesn't get out and about,' Kathleen said.

Emily poured more tea and added turf to the fire. She had forgotten to draw the curtains over and she did so now. The light in the room was dim; he'd been particular about low-wattage electric bulbs. But the dimness made the room cosy and it seemed wrong that anywhere should be so while he lay only a few hours dead. She wondered what she'd do when another bulb went, either here or somewhere else, if she would replace it with a stronger one or if low-wattage light was part of her now. She wondered if her nervousness was part of her too. It didn't seem that it had always been, but she knew she could be wrong about that.

'I didn't go out and about much,' she said because a silence in the conversation had come. Both visitors were stirring sugar into their tea. When their teaspoons were laid down, Norah said:

'There's some wouldn't bother with that.'

'He was a difficult man. People would have told you.'

They did not contradict that. They did not say anything. She said:

'He put his trust in the horses. Since childhood what he wanted was to win races, to be known for it. But he never managed much.'

'Poor man,' Kathleen murmured. 'Poor man.'

'Yes.'

She shouldn't have complained, she hadn't meant to: Emily tried to say that, but the words wouldn't come. She looked away from the women who had visited her, gazing about her at the furniture of a room she knew too well. He had been angry when she'd taken the curtains down to wash them; everyone staring in, he'd said, and she hadn't known what he'd meant. Hardly anyone passed by on the road.

'He married me for the house,' she said, unable to prevent herself from saying that too. The women were strangers, she was speaking ill of the dead. She shook her head in an effort to deny what she'd said, but that seemed to be a dishonesty, worse than speaking ill.

The women sipped their tea, both lifting the cups to their lips in the same moment.

'He married me for the forty acres,' Emily said, compelled again to say what she didn't want to. 'I was a Protestant girl that got passed by until he made a bid for me and I thought it was romantic, like he did himself – the race cards, the race ribbons, the jockeys' colours, the big crowd there'd be. That's how it happened.'

'Ah now, now,' Kathleen said. 'Ah now, dear.'

'I was a fool and you pay for foolishness. I was greedy for what marriage might be, and you pay for greed. We'd a half acre left after what was paid back a year ago. There's a mortgage he took out on the house.

I could have said to him all the time he was dying, "What'll I do?" But I didn't, and he didn't say anything either. God knows what his last thoughts were.'

They told her she was upset. One after the other they told her any widow would be, that it was what you had to expect. Norah said it twice. Kathleen said she could call on them in her grief.

'There's no grief in the house you've come to.'

'Ah now, now,' Kathleen said, her big face puckered in distress. 'Ah, now.'

'He never minded how the truth came out, whether he'd say it or not. He didn't say I was a worthless woman, but you'd see it in his eyes. Another time, I'd sweep the stable-yard and he'd say what use was that. He'd push a plate of food away untouched. We had two collies once and they were company. When they died he said he'd never have another dog. The vet wouldn't come near us. The man who came to read the meter turned surly under the abuse he got for driving his van into the yard.'

'There's good and bad in everyone, Emily.' Norah whispered that opinion and, still whispering, repeated it.

'Stay where you are, Emily,' Kathleen said, 'and I'll make another pot of tea.'

She stood up, the teapot already in her hand. She was used to making tea in other people's kitchens. She'd find her way about, she said.

Emily protested, but even while she did she didn't

care. In all the years of her marriage another woman hadn't made tea in that kitchen, and she imagined him walking in from the yard and finding someone other than herself there. The time she began to paint the scullery, it frightened her when he stood in the doorway, before he even said a thing. The time she dropped the sugar bag and the sugar spilt out all over the floor he watched her sweeping it on to the dustpan, turf dust going with it. He said what was she doing, throwing it away when it was still fit to stir into your tea? The scullery had stayed half-painted to this day.

'He lived in a strangeness of his own,' Emily said to the sister who was left in the room with her. 'Even when he was old, he believed a horse could still reclaim him. Even when the only one left was diseased and fit for nothing. When there was none there at all he scoured the empty stables and got fresh straw in. He had it in mind to begin all over again, to find some animal going cheap. He never said it, but it was what he had in mind.'

The house wasn't clean. It hadn't been clean for years. She'd lost heart in the house, and in herself, in the radio that didn't work, her bicycle with the tyres punctured. These visitors would have noticed that the summer flies weren't swept up, that nowhere was dusted.

'Three spoons and one for the pot,' Kathleen said, setting the teapot down in the hearth. 'Is that about right, Emily? Will we let it draw a minute?'

She had cut more brack, finding it on the breadboard, the bread saw beside it, the butter there too. She hoped it wasn't a presumption, she hoped it wasn't interference, she said, but all that remained unanswered.

'He'd sit there looking at me,' Emily said. 'His eyes would follow me about the kitchen. There was a beetle got on the table once and he didn't move. It got into the flour and he didn't reach out for it.'

'Isn't it a wonder,' Norah said, 'you wouldn't have gone off, the way things were, Emily? Not that I'm saying you should have.'

Emily was aware that that question was asked. She didn't answer it; she didn't know why she hadn't gone off. Looking back on it, she didn't. But she remembered how when she had thought of going away what her arguments to herself had been, how she had wondered where she could go to, and had told herself it would be wrong to leave a house that had been left to her in good faith and with affection. And then, of course, there was the worry about how he'd manage.

'Will you take another cup, Emily?'

She shook her head. The wind had become stronger. She could hear it rattling the doors upstairs. She'd left a light burning in the room.

'I'm wrong to delay you,' she said.

But the Geraghtys had settled down again, with the fresh tea to sustain them. She wasn't delaying them in any way whatsoever, Kathleen said. In the shadowy illumination of the single forty-watt bulb the alarm clock on the mantelpiece gave the time as twenty past eleven, although in fact it was half an hour later.

'It's just I'm tired,' Emily said. 'A time like this, I didn't mean to go on about what's done with.'

Kathleen said it was the shock. The shock of death changed everything, she said; no matter how certainly death was expected, it was always a shock.

'I wouldn't want you to think I didn't love my husband.'

The sisters were taken aback, Kathleen on her knees adding turf to the fire, Norah pouring milk into her tea. How could these two unmarried women understand? Emily thought. How could they understand that even if there was neither grief nor mourning there had been some love left for the man who'd died? Her fault, her foolishness from the first it had been; no one had made her do anything.

The talk went on, back and forth between the widow and the sisters, words and commiseration, solace and reassurance. The past came into it when more was said: the wedding, his polished shoes and shiny hair, the party afterwards over on the Curragh, at Jockey Hall because he knew the man there. People were spoken of, names known to the Geraghtys, or people before their time; occasions were spoken of – the year he went to Cheltenham, the shooting of the old grey when her leg went at Glanbyre point-to-point. The Geraghtys spoke of their growing up in Galway, how you wouldn't recognize the City of the Tribes these days so fashionable and lively it had become; how later they had lived near Enniscorthy; how Kathleen had felt the draw of the religious life at that time but then had felt the receding of it, how she had known ever since that she'd been tested with her own mistake. In this way the Geraghtys spread themselves into the conversation. As the night went on, Emily was aware that they were doing so because it was necessary, on a bleak occasion, to influence the bleakness in other ways. She apologized for speaking ill of the dead, and blamed herself again. It was half past three before the Geraghtys left.

'Thank you,' she said, holding open the hall door. The wind that had been slight and then had got up wasn't there any more. The air was fresh and clean. She said she'd be all right.

Light flickered in the car when the women opened the doors. There was the red glow of the tail-light before the engine started up, a whiff of exhaust before the car moved slowly forward and gathered speed.

*

In the room upstairs, the sheet drawn up over the raddled, stiffening features, Emily prayed. She knelt by the bedside and pleaded for the deliverance of the husband who had wronged her for so long. Fear had drained to a husk the love she had spoken of, but she did not deny that remnant's existence, as she had not in the company of her visitors. She could not grieve, she could not mourn; too little was left, too much destroyed. Would they know that as they drove away? Would they explain it to people when people asked?

Downstairs, she washed up the cups and saucers. She would not sleep. She would not go to bed. The hours would pass and then the undertaker's man would come.

*

The headlights illuminated low stone walls, ragwort thriving on the verges, gorse among the motionless sheep in gated fields. Kathleen drove, as she always did, Norah never having learnt how to. A visit had not before turned out so strangely, so different from what had been the sisters' familiar expectation. They said all that, and then were silent for a while before Kathleen made her final comment: that what they had heard had been all the more terrible to listen to with a man dead in an upstairs room.

Hunched in the dark of the car, Norah frowned over that. She did not speak immediately, but when they'd gone another mile she said:

'I'd say, myself, it was the dead we were sitting with.'

*

In the house the silence there had been before the visitors disturbed it was there again. No spectre rose from the carnal remains of the man who was at last at peace. But the woman sitting by the turf fire she kept going was aware, as dawn lightened the edges of the curtains, of a stirring in her senses. Her tiredness afflicted her less, a calm possessed her. In the neglected room she regretted nothing now of what she had said to the women who had meant well; nor did it matter if, here and there, they had not quite understood. She sat for a while longer, then pulled the curtains back and the day came in. Hers was the ghost the night had brought, in her own image as she once had been.

Traditions

They came in one by one as they always did. Hambrose, then Forrogale; Accrington, Olivier, Macluse, Newcombe, Napier. Each in turn saw the jackdaws dead on the earthen floor: seven, as there were seven of them.

'It's Leggett,' Macluse said and the others were silent. Only Napier also suspected Leggett. The others were bewildered, except for Olivier. The birds' necks had been snapped, one of the heads twisted off. Lying in the dust, their feathers already had a lank look; their beady gaze had dulled. 'Some bloody people,' Newcombe said flatly, his tone empty of protest or emotion. Olivier knew it was the girl.

A bell was chiming, calling them to Chapel. In the morning there was never longer than those few minutes, just time enough to get to the barn and make sure the birds were all right. Usually the chiming started when the seven were already on the way back. Earlier they'd had their morning smoke.

'Oh, *God!*' Macluse spat out as they hurried. Forrogale and Accrington said they now agreed: it was Leggett. No one else said anything.

They taught their birds to talk. Generations had before them. They enticed the very young ones; they clipped their wings and tamed them. There were other places where they might have kept them but the barn was the most suitable, spacious and empty, chicken-wire drawn over the aperture that was a kind of window, tacked on to the bottom of the doors. It was used for no other purpose, derelict and forgotten until a reminder that this whole area was out-of-bounds was again issued – an edict that regularly became forgotten also. So it had been for generations. But never before had there been a slaughter.

The jackdaws did not speak clearly when they were taught. They did not converse with one another, nor even release a single utterance that might be called a word. The sounds that came from them after hours of instruction were approximate, meaning interpreted by the listener. More satisfactory results might have been obtained, it was said, if the tongues were slit, and in the past that had been done, but not for many years now. It was felt to be not quite the thing.

With scarcely a minute to spare the seven boys arrived at the Chapel precincts, passed the line of masters waiting to make an entrance from the cloisters, and took their places, all of them sitting together. That something was wrong this morning was at once apparent to their peers; curiosity was whetted as prayers were mumbled, and hymns sung with roistering enthusiasm. The grave-faced chaplain conducted the service, briefly touching upon the temptations in the wilderness, since it was the time of year to do so. His gravity was a familiar quality in him, in no way caused by what had occurred in the night, which he did not know about. 'For it is written,' he quoted, 'He shall give his angels charge over thee.' Tidily with that, he brought his exposition to an end. As boys and masters, all formally gowned, filed back into the fresh air, the organ voluntary was by Handel.

There was a general dispersal while, increasing in volume, talk began. Boys went several ways, to widely scattered classrooms, the masters in one direction only, to collect from their common-room what books were immediately needed. Hambrose and Accrington remained together, as did Macluse and Napier and Newcombe, all three of whom belonged in a cleverer set. Forrogale had a piano lesson; Olivier had been summoned by the Headmaster. Each of the seven had on his mind the outrage that had occurred, and neither resentment nor anger had receded.

Forrogale practised while he waited, since he had not practised much in the time that had passed since he and Mr Hancock last had met. In the Headmaster's house the blue light above the drawing-room door was extinguished when the school butcher and handyman, Dynes, left the room. He winked at Olivier in a sinister manner, implying that he knew more than he did about Olivier's summons. The winking went unacknowledged, since it was one of Dynes's usual ploys. Olivier rapped lightly on a panel of the door and was told to come in.

'I am disappointed,' the Headmaster declared at once, leading the way from the fire against which he had been warming himself to a small adjoining room untidy with books and papers and confiscated objects. A burly, heavily made man, he sat down behind a desk while Olivier stood. 'Disappointed to note,' he went on, 'that you have failed to come up to scratch in any one of the three scientific subjects. Yet it seems you yourself had chosen the scientific side of things.' He broke off to peer at a piece of paper he had drawn towards him. 'Your ambitions are in that direction?'

'I was curious to know more about science, sir.'

'Sit down, Olivier.'

'Thank you, sir.'

'You say curious?'

'Yes, sir.'

'Now tell me why you are curious in that way. Remember I have a duty – and a conscience if I knowingly release upon the innocent world the ignorant and the inept. The fees at this school are high, Olivier. They are high because expectations are high. Your housemaster has said this to you. You are here this morning to be made aware of the seriousness we attach to it. When you went on to the scientific side you were not driven by vocation?'

'No, sir.'

'You indulged a curiosity. You indulged yourself: that can be dangerous.'

Why did the man have to speak in that pompous,

prissy way? Olivier asked himself. If it was self-indulgence simply to wish to learn more since he knew so little, then it was self-indulgence. In what way dangerous? he wondered, but did not ask. That he had failed to perform adequately in the laboratory had not surprised him, nor did it now.

He said he was sorry, and the Headmaster spoke of the school's belief in tradition, which he did on all convenient occasions. What he extolled had little, if anything at all, to do with Olivier's failure. That this was so was a tradition in itself, all deviations from required behaviour assumed to have a source in careless disregard of time-hardened precepts and mores. This Headmaster's predecessors had in their day advocated such attention to the past, to the achievements of boys when they became men, to the debts they owed. In turn, Olivier's predecessors had listened with the same degree of scepticism and disdain.

'Shall we put it like this,' the present Headmaster suggested, 'that you promise me this morning to knuckle down? That we review the circumstances in, say, five weeks' time?'

'Or I could give up science, sir.'

'Give up? I hardly like the sound of that.'

'I made a mistake, sir.'

'Do not compound it, Olivier. Failure is a punishment in itself. Perhaps you might dwell on that?'

With this suggestion Olivier was dismissed. In the great stone-paved hall beyond the study and the drawing-room he forgot at once all that had been said and returned to the subject of the slaughtered birds. Again he reached the conclusion he had reached already: that the culprit was not another boy. Leggett would be seized after the games practices this afternoon and accused under duress. Dawdling on the journey to his classroom, Olivier anticipated that unfair revenge but knew he would still not reveal what he suspected. There was pleasure in not doing so, in holding things back, in knowing what others didn't.

★

Wednesdays until tea were hers. They always had been and she would have hated a change. That middle-of-the-week day she had come to regard as her private Sunday – when her alarm didn't go off, when the Chapel bell and First School bell, sounding in the distance, could be ignored. Even her unconscious knew what to do: to sleep on until the morning was half gone. It was ragged sleep, made restless with dreams that were always vivid at this time, but that never mattered. Nothing was more luxurious than Wednesday mornings, than imagining between dozing and waking the untidy after-breakfast dining hall, and the silence that came suddenly when classes began, the cutlery carried to the pantries, polished clean there, carried back again, the big oak tables laid for lunch. She had Saturday evening off as well but it wasn't the same, nothing much really and often she stood in for one of the others, not even wanting to be paid back.

She rose this morning at half past ten, her usual Wednesday time. She read a colour supplement while the kettle boiled. She opened the back door and stood there in her nightdress, shooing away the cat that was a nuisance. Stacpoole used to come to her on Wednesday mornings, the only one who ever had, the only one who in all the years had ever managed to have a free period then, eleven to a quarter to twelve. She remembered Stacpoole returning to the school long afterwards with a woman they said would be his wife, pointing out to her this place or that. She remembered wondering if she'd been pointed out herself.

She stood a little longer, relishing the soft, fresh air. Then the smell of toast drew her back into her kitchen.

*

They made coffee in the quarry and drank it out of jampots. They drank it very sweet but without milk because milk was a nuisance. Then, lying on their backs in the sun, they smoked.

Leggett, meanwhile, crept back to his House, simulating lameness for as long as he estimated he could be seen. He thought he had a cracked rib but Forrogale, claiming medical knowledge, had said no, having poked it with his fingers. 'Definitely not,' Forrogale had said, but Leggett was not sure about that. They'd picked on him because he was underhand: they'd said so, and Leggett knew he was. None the less, he was innocent. He wouldn't have touched one of their hideous jackdaws, much less taken in his hand a head with a beak that could snap at you.

'He didn't do it,' Accrington said, breaking a long silence, and one at a time the others agreed. Not that duffing up Leggett was in the least to be regretted.

'Who?' Napier asked, and Olivier didn't say the girl.

'Unless it was Dynes,' Macluse said.

They all thought about that except Olivier. Dynes was outside the order of things; they could not duff him up or in any way harass him; they could not so much as speak to him about the matter, for although the handyman was aware that jackdaws were kept he would most likely counter the accusation by revealing what he had previously been silent about. He was a touchy man.

'I doubt in any case it was Dynes,' Accrington said. 'This doesn't have Dynes's fingerprints.'

Some years ago a boy had hanged himself but had not succeeded in taking his life. It was established afterwards that he had not intended to, since the noose he had prepared had never tightened, one foot pressed into a hollow in the tree he'd chosen taking all the weight. The boy had not, though, remained at the school but had been sent home, considered unbalanced. This was spoken of now, since it was surely some similar individual who had killed the birds. The names of the unstable were bandied about, recent behaviour of new suspects discussed. Olivier remained silent. He was the smallest of the boys though not the youngest, his dark hair in a fringe above a sallow complexion. His looks stood out among those of his companions, a delicacy about him that the others could not claim. There was – or so it seemed when Olivier was there as an example of how it might be better done – a carelessness in how the others had been made. Adolescence was marked in them by jacket sleeves too short, unruly hair and coarsened voices, blemished skin beneath beginners' stubble. Yet none particularly noticed that Olivier had escaped this prelude to man's estate, the gangling awkwardness that his friends accepted without regret for what was left behind.

The last of the coffee was drunk, cigarette butts thrown into the embers of the fire before the charred remains of sticks were scattered. In a body, the boys returned to the school, then to the barn that had been their jackdaws' home. Hambrose, who knew the conventions of the school's farm through assisting in the work there, made a detour to collect a spade and advised on where it was best to dig a common grave. One by one the birds were dropped into it. Macluse piled back the clay and then the capturing of replacement birds began.

★

Long before Olivier came to the school there had been incidents in the past that word of mouth had since made famous: the ringing of the Chapel bell in the middle of the night; the removal of a Renoir print – 'Young Girl Reading' – from its place between the windows in one of the prefects' common-rooms; the purloining of a cigarette lighter and a pipe from a pocket of Dobie-Gordon's overcoat; the mysterious collapse of the central-heating system. Occurring over many years, the incidents had in common only that no culprit had ever been brought to book; nor did it seem possible that the same hand could have been responsible for any two of the occurrences – let alone all of them – since the length of a boy's stay at the school did not allow it. Seven years ago – long before Olivier's arrival – there'd been the trouble in the bicycle sheds: the random deflating of tyres. Then nothing had happened until the killing of the jackdaws.

It was purely intuition that caused Olivier to suspect the girl, not just of the latest outrage but of the others too. And though certain that he was right, so sure was his instinct, so unassailable his sensing of a purpose in all this, he could not think why one of the dining-hall maids should wish to alert the school to fire at one o'clock in the morning or what possible use she could have had for Dobie-Gordon's pipe. Somewhere here there was revenge, he had conjectured when first he'd had his idea, but had since rejected the speculation, for he considered it too pat and obvious. He thought so again on the day of Leggett's duffing up when at teatime he stared at the girl, trying to catch her when she wasn't looking. He was skilled at breaking into privacies without the knowledge of the person observed; he prided himself on that, but twice, or even three times, he suddenly had to drop his scrutiny, taken unawares by having his gaze returned. Bella this maid's name was, but 'the girl' identified her in the dining hall and beyond it.

Along one arm, plates touching to keep them balanced, the dining-hall maids could carry five at a time, each bearing a sausage roll, or toast with beans or scrambled eggs. Today it was sausage roll, two sausages in each envelope of pastry, the pastry dark brown and flaky. At St Andrew's Second Table you passed your sausage roll to Chom, who ate it for you. Elsewhere in the dining hall more usual conventions prevailed, unwanted sausage rolls disposed of later.

Olivier's place this evening at St David's Third Table was on the prefect's right, a position that recurred every twelve days, each boy but for the prefect moving on a place each day. The prefect did not speak except to request the salt or pepper or jam; it was his privilege to be aloof. The warm plates were passed along each row of boys, the prefect's fetched at the last moment and mustard brought with it.

The maid who interested Olivier did not serve this table. He watched her at the far end of the dining hall, where the St Patrick's tables were, where Accrington and Newcombe and Hambrose sat. Only Olivier, among the boys who tamed jackdaws, was in St David's. Forrogale and Macluse and Napier were in St George's, the House renowned for games.

The noise in the dining hall was considerable, but the only snatches of conversation that reached Olivier were from his own table, all else being lost in the general din. The Saturday-evening debate this week was to be about the existence or otherwise of ghosts. This was talked about in advance; and an item of national news – the conviction of a medical doctor who had murdered a number of his female patients – was discussed, the death penalty advocated or opposed. Olivier drank his tea and passed his cup and saucer to where a large metal teapot was in the charge of the two boys at the table's other end. Then he watched the maid again. Waiting for the moment when the clearing away of plates and cutlery began, she stood now in a line with the other maids in front of the high table, which was unoccupied during this meal.

She was a girl in name only, a designation that carried from the past, from when she had been the youngest of the maids by many years. It honoured a celebrity she had enjoyed, when her fresh beauty had time and again inspired passion in the dining hall. Such facts came into the mystery of the incidents, Olivier felt himself guessing; but did not know how. She did not mind being observed: that, too, was there.

'Olivier,' the prefect interrupted the blankness that followed these reflections. 'Jam.'

Olivier reached for the dish of apple jam, apologizing. She was a woman in late middle age now, tall, with grey hair tied back behind her cap, her features still touched with a trace of the beauty other boys had known. Olivier understood – had come to understand when first he'd been interested in her – why she was different from the other maids. It was not just the tales that lingered from the past, nor the reminder in her features that these were not exaggerated, nor her preference for silence when the other maids chattered in carefully guarded dining-hall whispers. There was something else, belonging only to her. Again her glance caught his, too far away for Olivier to be certain that it did so intentionally, but he was certain anyway.

The grey sausage meat within his pastry smelt a bit; not that it was bad, Olivier knew, for the smell was of sausage and of meat; only that the cooking had drawn some excess of natural odour from it. The first time she'd looked in his direction he hadn't recognized her and would have passed her by because she wasn't in her uniform. Often since, he'd noticed her on the back drive, alone on her afternoon off or when her duties for the day were done, not in a bunch as the others usually were. She never smiled, nothing like that, and he didn't himself.

There was the clatter of standing up, the benches pushed back from the tables, the shuffling of shoes on polished boards. '... *per Christum Dominum nostrum,*' the Senior Prefect intoned and then there were the evening's announcements, the duty master hurrying off, the prefects going when the announcements finished, one falling in behind another, interrupted conversations picked up as the dining hall emptied but for the maids.

It would not be the birds again. There was always a variation, and Olivier had once tried to guess what the next transgression would be, but had failed hopelessly. He would not be here when it occurred, and he imagined returning for some Old Boys' event and hearing something casually mentioned. He imagined not quite knowing what had happened and having to ask outright in the end. For a moment he wanted to reassure his friends that the new birds were safe, that there would not be a repetition. But he desisted. It was a time for cigarettes again, and the seven trooped off to the stone hut they had built for that purpose, out of sight in a corner of a field.

That evening the Headmaster himself spoke at compline, which on rare occasions he did. He told a parable of his own invention: how a man, repeating every day of his life a certain pattern of behaviour, made the pattern richer. He told of how, in a dream, this man had deviated once from his chosen way and been harshly judged by God, and punished with failure where all his life there had been success before.

Olivier recognized in the words a faintly apposite

note and wondered if inspiration for them had perhaps come from his own deviation, and subsequent failure, in the realm of science. In ending his address, the Headmaster did not omit to include a reference to the value of tradition, claiming for it and for the school it ruled a potency that must surely be the approval of the God who punished when displeased. The Headmaster's philosophy did not vary except in the allegorical garb of his discourse. It was a circle that came full, ending where it had begun: with the school and its time-worn customs, tried and true, that made men of boys.

Later, in scanning a Horace ode with the aid of a Kelly's Key, Olivier found himself distracted, in turn, by the Headmaster's overwhelming confidence in the established rites of passage through his school and by the dining-hall maid's transgressions. Were her sins the weaponry of insurrection, intended as such or simply so because they happened? What passed through her thoughts as she implemented another disturbance or discomfort? And why was it that the Headmaster's beliefs and a woman's recidivistic stratagems seemed now to cling together like proximate jigsaw pieces? *Angustam amice pauperiem pati, robustus acri militia puer condiscat*, Horace had written; and Olivier matched Latin and English as best he could, his key's translation not being word for word.

Of course, the Headmaster did not know – as authority before him had not known – that the dining-hall maid had in her girlhood been, herself, a fragment of tradition, supplying to boys who now were men a service that had entered the unofficial annals. There was that too, Olivier reminded himself, before he returned to winkling out which word went with which.

⋆

At the end of the day the dining-hall maids, and the dormitory maids, and those with diverse duties, went home, some sharing the available space in the cars that a few of them drove, others on bicycles, some on foot to the village. Among those who walked was the girl who was now a woman. She smoked on the leafy back drive, a little behind two of her colleagues, one of whom lit the way with a torch. The skin of the boy she admired was still as smooth as porcelain though not as white, and without the blush of pink that porcelain flesh went in for. She loved the sallow tinge, the dark eyes gazing out of it, the fringe that so perfectly followed the forehead's contour.

His image filled her consciousness as she walked on, his voice the voice of boys who had long ago tenderly spoken her name. He knew, as she had guessed he would be the one to know, because he was the kind. She'd always known the kind.

⋆

The first of the late bells sounded, rhythmically clang-
ing. Younger boys gathered up their books, and then
their footsteps were muffled in the corridors, no conversation exchanged because noise was forbidden while
the Upper and Middle School classes continued their
preparation. Olivier read *Cakes and Ale*, the orange-
backed book hidden from view behind *Raleigh and the
British Empire* and a guide to laboratory experiments.
Was it Chapman, do you think? a note interrupted this,
passed along the row of desks to him. *Maybe*, he
scribbled and passed the scrap of paper back to Newcombe. You had to lie. They'd be suspicious if you kept
denying it whenever they mentioned anyone.

Someone would guess: one after another she had
caused the incidents to happen so that someone would
guess. As certain as he was about everything else, so
he was certain that this last conjecture was not fanciful.
He knew no more; he doubted that he ever would. In
his mind's eye he saw her as once or twice he had
when he'd been out and about at this time himself: in
her navy-blue coat, the belt tied loosely, a headscarf
with horses on it.

*

'Cheers, Bella,' the two in front called out, one after
the other, as they turned into Parsley Lane. 'Cheers.'

She loathed that cheap word, so meaningless, used
all the time now. 'Good night,' she called back.

Voices and the occasional laugh accompanied the bobbing torchlight in Parsley Lane. She went a different way and heard only the hooting of an owl. She came to the Railwayman, where there were voices and laughter again, and then the television turned loud in Mrs Hodges' front room.

Her mother, still alive, would be in her bed: she pretended that. And he would be silent among the churchyard yews, and would say nothing while she went by. Then when she had brought the tea upstairs and had sat a while to watch the old eyelids droop, she'd slide back the wooden bolt and move the curtain an inch to the right, leaving it for just a moment. He would come in without a knock.

Someone leaving the Railwayman called after her, saying good night, and she called back. She could have had any of them; she still could, for all she knew. My God, she thought, the stifled life it would have been, with any one of them!

She didn't mind the short cut by the churchyard, not any more. She'd passed through the lines of gravestones too often, the Greshams' great family vault damaged and open in one place, the smashed, forgotten wreaths eerie when there was moonlight. The odour she'd once associated with the dead was old leaves rotting.

The cottage where all her life she'd lived was the last in the village. Her father had left it every morning of her childhood to go to work at the quarry; he'd died upstairs, where her mother had too. A boy had come on the day her mother died and she'd had to send him away, head of St Andrew's he'd been, Tateman. *La même chose*: it was he who'd taught her that, and *chacun à son goût*, making her pout her lips to get the sounds. Long afterwards she'd imagined travelling with him, all over France and Germany, saying *la même chose* herself when she was offered a dessert, wanting what he'd had. Fair-haired he'd been, not at all like the present one, whose name she did not know.

She turned the latchkey in her front door and drew the curtains in the room she'd walked straight into, the heavy one over the door to keep the draught out. Two bars of the electric fire warmed her ankles when she sat down, with tea and Petit Beurre. The secret side of it they'd always relished, as much as the other in a way. And she had, too – not quite as much but almost.

*

When the dormitory had quietened Olivier thought about her again. He wondered how, when she was young, her expression had changed when her mood did. He imagined her demure, for there was about her sometimes in the dining hall a trace of that as she stood waiting for Grace to be said, while the others were impatient. Conjecturing again, he saw her in a different coat, without a headscarf, hair blown about. He saw her uniform laid out, starched and ready on an ironing board, a finger damped before the iron's heat was tested. He saw her stockinged feet and laughter in her eyes, and then her nakedness.

Justina's Priest

Only Justina Casey made sense, Father Clohessy
reflected yet again, shaking his head over the recur-
rence of the thought, for truth to tell the girl made no
sense at all. The contradiction nagged a little in a
familiar way, as it did whenever Justina Casey, sinless
as ever, made her confession. It caused Father Clohessy
to feel inadequate, foolish even, that he failed to understand something that as a priest he should have.

Leaving the confessional she had just left herself, he
looked around for her: at the back, near the holy-water
stoup, she trailed her rosary through her fingers.
'Father, I'm bad,' she had insisted and, allotting her her
penance, he had been again aware that she didn't even
know what badness was. But without the telling of her
beads, without the few Hail Marys he had prescribed,
she would have gone away unhappy. Of her own vol-
ition, every few days she polished the brass of the altar
vases and the altar cross. She would be there on Saturday
evening, a bucket of scalding water carried through
the streets, the floor mop lifted down from its hook in
the vestry cupboard. On Fridays she scraped away the
week's accumulation of candle grease and arranged to
her satisfaction the out-of-date missionary leaflets.

Fifty-four and becoming stout, his red hair cut short around a freckled pate, Father Clohessy watched while Justina Casey dipped the tips of her fingers in the holy water and blessed herself before she left the church. Her footsteps were soft on the tiles, as if her devotion demanded that, as if she were of less importance than the sacred ground she walked on, less than the burning candles and the plaster Virgin, less even than the unread missionary leaflets. He remembered her at her First Communion, standing out a bit from the other children, a scraggy bunch of lily-of-the-valley pressed close to her. It was afterwards that she'd asked him if she could look after the brass.

The door of the church closed soundlessly behind her and Father Clohessy was aware of an emptiness, of something taken from him.

*

Justina dawdled, examining the goods in the shop windows. There were the tins of sweets in Hehir's, and the glass jars in a row behind them, half full of the mixtures, the jelly babies and bull's-eyes, soft-centred fruits, toffees. There were the fashions in Merrick's, the window changed only a week ago, meat in Cranly's, delft and saucepans in Natton's. A fine dust had gathered on the dry goods in MacGlashan's, on packets of Barry's tea and the advertisements for Bisto and chicken-and-ham paste. Cabbage drooped outside Mrs Scally's, the green fringe of the carrots was tinged with yellow.

'How's Justina?' Mrs Scally enquired from the door-way, the flowered overall that encased her girth crossed over on itself beneath her folded arms. She always had her arms folded, Justina's thought was as she stopped to hear what else Mrs Scally had to say. One shoulder taking the weight against the door-jamb, a single curler left in her hair, slippers on her feet and the folded arms: that was Mrs Scally unless she was weighing out potatoes or wrapping a turnip. 'All right,' Justina said. 'I'm all right, Mrs Scally.'

'I have apples in. Will you tell them up in the house I have apples in?'

'I will.'

'There's a few tins of peaches that's dinged. I wouldn't charge the full.'

'You told me that, Mrs Scally.'

'Did you mention it in the house?'

'I did surely.'

Justina passed on. She had spoken to Maeve about the peaches and her sister hadn't said anything. But Mr Gilfoyle had heard her saying it and he'd laughed. When Micksie came in he said that if the dinge in the tin caused rust you'd have to be careful. Micksie was Maeve's husband, Mr Gilfoyle was his father. Diamond Street was where they lived, where Maeve ruled the small household and most of the time was unable to hide the fact that she resented its composition. Cap-able and brisk of manner, a tall, dark-haired childless woman, Maeve considered that she'd been caught: when their mother had died there had been only she to look after Justina, their mother being widowed for as long as either of them could remember. And Maeve had been caught again when her father-in-law, miserable with the ailments of old age, had to be taken in; and again in not realizing before her marriage that Micksie had to be kept out of the pubs. 'Oh, I have children all right,' was how she often put it when there was sympathy for her childlessness.

Justina bought an ice-cream in the Today Tonight shop. The evening papers had just come off the Dublin bus. *No-vote a Winner*, the headline said and she wondered what that meant. People she knew were gathering items from the shelves, minerals in bottles and tins, frozen food from the central refrigerator, magazines from the racks. She walked about, licking at her ice-cream, nibbling the edge of the cone. Up one aisle and down another, past shoe polish and disinfectant and fire-lighters, carton soups reduced, everything handy in case you'd forgotten to get it in Superquinn.

'You're a great girl,' one of two nuns remarked, reaching out for Kerrygold and dropping it into her wire basket. Older and more severe, the other nun didn't say anything.

'Ah, I'm not,' Justina said. She held out her ice-cream, but neither nun licked it. 'No way I'm great,' Justina said.

★

'What kept you?' Maeve asked in the kitchen.

'Mrs Scally was on about the peaches. Sister Agnes and Sister Lull were in the Today Tonight.'

'What'd you go in there for?'

'Nothing.'

Justina paused for an instant and then she told about the ice-cream and Maeve knew it was because her sister had suddenly considered it would be a lie to hold that back.

'God, will you look at the cut of you!' She shouted, furious, unable to help herself. 'Aren't there jobs to do here without you're streeling about the town?'

'I had to make my confession.'

'Oh, for heaven's sake!'

'What's up, Maeve?'

Maeve shook her head. She could feel a weariness in her eyes which made her want to close them, and then felt it spreading through her body. She returned to what she'd been doing before Justina came in, slicing cooked potatoes.

'Lay the table,' she said. 'Take your anorak off and lay the table.'

'I got a letter from Breda,' Justina said.

She had closed the back door behind her but hadn't come further into the kitchen. She had a way of doing that, just as she had a way of standing by the sink, not getting on with what she was there for, as if she'd forgotten everything. All their lives, for as long as Maeve could remember, she had been irritated by this shortcoming in her sister, as she was by Justina's bringing back messages from the shopkeepers to say this or that commodity had come in or that there was a new bargain line, as she was by the telephone calls that came from a farmer nearly six miles from the town to say that Justina was again feeding his bullocks bunches of grass. Not that he objected, the man always said, only the bullocks could be frisky and maybe crowd her.

'Will you read me Breda's letter, Maeve?'

'You keep away from that one, d'you hear me?'

'Sure, Breda's gone.'

'And she'll stay where she is.'

'Will I lay the table, Maeve?'

'Didn't I ask you to?'

'I'll lay it so.'

★

Father Clohessy walked in the opposite direction from the one taken by Justina. The sense of loss that had possessed him when she left the church had given way to a more general feeling of deprivation that, these days, he was not often without. The grandeur of his Church had gone, leaving his priesthood within it bleak, the vocation that had beckoned him less insistent than it had been. He had seen his congregations fall off and struggled against the feeling that he'd been deserted. Confusion spread from the mores of the times into the

Church itself; in combating it, he prayed for guidance but was not heard.

A familiar melancholy, not revealed in his manner, accompanied Father Clohessy in the minutes it took him to reach the limestone figure of the rebel leader in the square that was the centre of the town. That he considered it necessary to keep private his concern about the plight of his Church did nothing to lighten the burden of his mood, any more than the temporary absence from the parish of Father Finaghy did. At present undergoing a period of treatment after a car accident, Father Finaghy was extrovert and gregarious, a priest who carried his faith on to the golf-course, where it was never a hindrance. 'Arrah, sure we do our best,' Father Finaghy was given to remarking. Father Clohessy missed his companionship; almost a protection it seemed like sometimes.

'Have you change, Father?' a young woman begged from a doorway, a baby asleep in a shawl beside her. 'A few coppers at all today?'

She said she'd pray for him and he thanked her, finding the coins she hoped for. He knew her; she was usually there. He might have asked her when he'd see her at Mass, but he didn't bother.

Music blared across the small square from Mulvany's Electrical and TV, giving way to the careless whine of Bob Dylan. Mulvany had established for himself a tradition of celebrating the birthdays of popular entertainers by playing a tribute: today Bob Dylan was sixty.

Although one song only was played on these occasions, and no more than once during the day it related to, Father Clohessy considered it a disturbance in a quiet town and had once approached Mulvany about it. But Mulvany had argued that it was nostalgic for the older citizens to hear the likes of Perry Como or Dolly Parton coming out of the blue at them, and exciting for the youngsters to have the new arrivals on the music scene honoured. That a priest's protest had been so summarily dismissed was par for the course, an expression often used by Father Finaghy in his own unprotesting acceptance of the decline of clerical influence. The times they were a-changing, Bob Dylan's reminder was repeated yet again before there was silence from Mulvany's loudspeakers.

'Isn't that a grand day, Father?' a woman remarked to him and he agreed that it was and she said thank God for it. He wondered if she knew, if any of them knew, that when he preached he was angry because he didn't know what to say to them, that he searched for ways to disguise his distress, stumbling about from word to word. 'How's Father Finaghy?' the woman asked him. 'Have you heard, Father?'

He told her. Father Finaghy was making good progress; he'd heard that morning.

'Wouldn't it be the prayers said for him?' the woman suggested, and he agreed with that, too, before he resumed his journey through the town to where he and Father Finaghy lodged.

His tea was ready for him there. Comeraghview, called after the mountains in the faraway distance, was a grey detached house with a handkerchief tree in a front garden protected from the main road by grey iron railings. It was he and Father Finaghy who had decided that the presbytery could be put to better use, who with their bishop's permission, and in the end with his blessing, had given it over to become the youth centre the town had long been in need of.

'I have ham and a salad for you,' Father Clohessy's landlady said, placing this food in front of him.

★

'I will of course,' Mr Gilfoyle said when Justina asked him to read Breda Maguire's letter to her. 'Have you it there?'

Justina had, and Mr Gilfoyle suggested that they'd take it out the back where they'd be private. His daughter-in-law went ballistic at any mention of Breda Maguire these days, never mind having to hear of her doings in Dublin. Time was when someone who'd take her sister off her hands was a relief for Maeve, but now that the two girls were grown up and Breda Maguire had gone off the rails it was naturally different.

'*I'm living in a great joint!*' he read aloud in the small flowerless back garden that had become a depository for the abandoned wash-basins and lavatory bowls and perforated ballcocks that his son had replaced in his work as a plumber. Nettles had grown up around cast-iron heating radiators and a bath; dandelions and docks flourished. Mr Gilfoyle had cleared a corner, where he kept a chair from the kitchen; on sunny mornings he read the newspaper there.

He was a moustached man, grey-haired, once burly and on the stout side, less so now, since time had established in him the varying characteristics of advancing years. His pronounced stoop, an arthritic shoulder, trouble with gallstones, fingers distorted by Dupuytren's Disease had made another man of him. In his day he, too, had been a plumber.

'*The kind of house you wouldn't know about*,' he read out, imagining what was described: a place where theatre people lived, coffee always on the go, late mornings. Mr Gilfoyle found it hard to believe that Breda Maguire had been given accommodation there, but he supposed it could be true.

Justina, sitting on the edge of the bath, had no such difficulty. She accepted without demur all that was related. She saw her friend in the green-and-blue kimono that was described. '*Like a dragon wrapped round me*,' Mr Gilfoyle had read out and explained that a kimono was Japanese. He felt what he believed to be a gallstone changing position inside him somewhere, a twitch of pain that was only to be expected at his age he'd been told by the doctor he visited regularly.

'*Davy Byrne's you'd never see only it's jammed to the*

doors. *The racing crowd, all that kind of thing.'* Breda
Maguire was on the streets, Mr Gilfoyle said to himself.
She had money, you could tell she had, nothing made
up about that. The house she said she was stopping in
was out Islandbridge way and again there was an echo
of the truth in that, handy for the quays. The quays
were where you'd find them, a bricklayer told him
once, maybe fifty years ago, and it could still be where
a man would go to look for a street woman. *'I have a
friend takes me out,'* he read. *'Billy.'*

'Will you listen to that!' Justina whispered. The name
of a hotel where there were dances was mentioned,
shops, cinemas. A wrist bangle had been bought, and
Justina saw her friend and Billy at a counter with a
glass top like the one in Hennessy's the Clock Shop,
necklaces and bangles laid out for them. She saw them
in a café, a waitress bringing grills, the same as Justina
had seen people eating in Egan's, a chop and chips,
bacon, egg and sausage. Billy was like the air pilot in
the film she and Breda had watched on the television
only the day before Breda went off. *'How's tricks with
yourself?'* Mr Gilfoyle's voice continued.

It would be impossible for Justina to respond to that
because her learning difficulty deprived her of any
communication that involved writing words down.
But Breda had remembered, as naturally she would.
'I'll maybe give you a call one of these days,' Mr Gilfoyle
read out. The pain had shifted, had gone round to the
back, like a gallstone maybe would.

'Isn't Billy great, the way he'd give her things?'
Justina said.

'He is, Justina.'

'Isn't Billy a great name?'

'It is.'

Covering a multitude of sins, Mr Gilfoyle assumed,
a stand-in name for names Breda didn't know, the
presents another way of putting it that money had
changed hands in some quayside doorway.

'I'll dream about Breda and Billy,' Justina said,
slipping down from the edge of the bath.

★

Father Clohessy listened when Justina put it into her
confession that Maeve was cross with her because Breda
telephoned. She put it into her confession that she went
into the kitchen to tell what Breda had said and Maeve
wouldn't listen; and the next thing was she let drop a cup
she was drying. It was then that Maeve began to cry,
tears streaming down her cheeks, down her neck into
the collar of her dress. As if it wasn't nuisance enough,
an old man who didn't know how to make his bed
forever on about his ailments. As if it wasn't enough,
Micksie in and out of the pubs, a girl with learning
trouble, the back garden a tip. Was there a woman
in Ireland could put up with more, when on top of
everything a hooer the like of Breda Maguire got going
again after they thought they'd seen the back of her?

All that Justina put into her confession. She was bad,
she said. One minute she was laughing with Breda on
the phone; the next, Maeve was crying in the kitchen.
Breda said come up to Dublin and they'd have great
gas. Get the money however, Breda said. Get it off
Mr Gilfoyle, anything at all. Take the half-two bus, the
same as she'd got herself. Come up for the two days,
what harm would it do anyone? 'I'll show you the
whole works,' Breda said.

The fingers of Father Clohessy's hands were locked
together as he listened, that being his usual pose in the
confessional, head turned so that one ear could pick up
the revelations that were coming through the gauze of
the grille. Among his confessants, it was only Justina
he ever interrupted and he did so now.

'Ah no, Justina, no,' he said.

'Will I say a Hail Mary for Maeve, Father?'

'You wouldn't want to go up to Dublin, Justina. You
wouldn't want to upset your sister more.'

'It's only Breda's gone up there.'

'I know, I know.'

When they were no more than five or six he remembered the two of them playing in Diamond Street,
Justina's black hair cut in a fringe and curling in around
her face, Breda as thin as a weasel. She'd been the bane
of the nuns when she'd attended the convent, sly and
calculating, all knowing talk and unspoken defiance.
She'd plastered herself with lipstick when she was older;
in the end she'd worn a T-shirt with an indecency on it.

'Would it be bad to go up on the bus, Father?'

'I think maybe it would. Have you anything else to confess, Justina?'

'Only Maeve was crying.'

'Light a candle when you'll leave the confessional. Do the floor on Saturday, do the brasses.'

Again he remembered her standing on her own by the shrine outside the church after her First Communion, her face held up to the sunshine, the lily-of-the-valley tightly clenched. Before she left the confessional he murmured a prayer for her, knowing that was what she liked to hear best of all. It frightened him that she might visit her friend, that she might forget what he had said, that somehow she might acquire the bus fare, that she'd go, not telling anyone.

*

Two days later, when Justina was washing the church floor, Father Clohessy called at the house in Diamond Street.

'Come in, Father, come in,' Mr Gilfoyle said.

He led the way into a room where a football match was in progress on the television, Aston Villa and Arsenal. His son had been watching it, Mr Gilfoyle said, but then a call had come through, a tank overflowing on the McCarron estate. Mr Gilfoyle turned the football off. Maeve had gone out for rashers. She'd be back in no time, he said.

They talked about a job Mr Gilfoyle had done years ago in the church, putting in a sink in the vestry. Father Clohessy said it was still going strong; in use all the time, he said.

'A Belfast sink,' Mr Gilfoyle said. 'A Belfast sink was the name we had for that fellow. You wouldn't see the better of it.'

'No.'

'Sit down, Father. I have to sit down myself. I have trouble in the old legs.'

A sound came from the kitchen. Mr Gilfoyle called out to his daughter-in-law that Father Clohessy was here and when Maeve came in, still in her coat, a scarf tied round her hair, Father Clohessy said:

'I wanted a word about Justina.'

'She's being a nuisance to you?'

'Ah no, no.'

'She lives in that church.'

'Justina's welcome, Maeve. No, it's only she was mentioning Breda Maguire. I'm concerned in case Justina might try to make her way to Dublin.'

There was a silence then. The priest was aware of Mr Gilfoyle being about to say something and changing his mind, and of Maeve's unbelieving stare. He watched while she restrained herself: once or twice before, she had been abrupt to the point of rudeness when he'd been concerned about her sister. He didn't say anything himself; the silence went on.

'She never would,' Maeve said at last.

Successful in controlling her irritation, she failed to keep an errant note of hope out of her tone. It flickered in her eyes and she shook her head, as if to deny that it was there.

'How could she, Father?'

'The bus goes every day.'

'She'd need money. She spends every penny soon as she gets it.'

'I just thought I'd say. So you could keep an eye on her.'

Maeve did not respond to that. Mr Gilfoyle said Justina would never board that bus. He'd walk down to the square himself and keep a look-out where the bus drew in.

'It would be worse if she got a lift off someone.'

Wearily, Maeve closed her eyes when Father Clohessy said that. She sighed and turned away, struggling with her anger, and Father Clohessy felt sorry for her. It wasn't easy, she did her best.

'We'll keep an eye on her,' she said.

★

That night, when Father Clohessy closed his church after the late Saturday Mass, he wondered if he had become prey to despair, the worst sin of all in the canon that was specially a priest's. At street corners, in the square, men stood in conversation, lit cigarettes, argued the chances of Offaly the next day. Women linked arms, talking as they strolled. Children carried away chips from O'Donnell's. The grandeur might have gone from his church, his congregations dwindling, his influence fallen away to nothing, but there was money where there'd been poverty, ambition where there'd been humility. These were liberated people who stood about in ways that generations before them had not. They wore what they wished to wear, they said what they wished to say, they stayed or went away. Was it much of a price to pay that the woman he had visited would rid herself of a backward sister if she could? It was on a Saturday evening little different from this one that he had first read the legend on Breda Maguire's T-shirt, bold yellow letters on black, simple and straightforward: *Fuck Me*.

On the streets of the town he had always known, people spoke to him, warmly, with respect. They wished him good night, they wished him well. He could not blame them if in his sermons he didn't know what to say to them any more. He should apologize, yet knew he must not. In the square, he entered the Emmet Bar, between the old Munster and Leinster Bank, now an AIB branch, and Mulvany's television shop. Father Finaghy always called in on Saturdays after they closed the church, and he sometimes did himself – to drink a couple of glasses of Beamish's stout and smoke a couple of cigarettes while he talked to two men with whom he had attended the Christian Brothers' forty years ago. Both had done well enough in the new prosperity, had fathered children and seen them educated, were decent men. He liked them as much as he always had, even sometimes was envious of their uncomplicated lives. They, not he, did the talking in the Emmet Bar, always sensitive to the cloth he wore. They neither of them had mentioned it when a few years ago a well-loved bishop had been exposed as the begetter of a child, nor when there had been other misdemeanours on the part of other clergymen.

'Bring us the same, Larry,' the bulkier of the two called out, a brightly coloured tie loosened in his collar, freckles darkening his forehead. Clumsy hands pushed the empty glasses across the bar. 'And one for the Father.'

'I wouldn't see Offaly victorious,' his companion remarked, tidier, wiry, a salesman of agricultural implements. 'No way.'

Music was faint in the crowded bar, as if coming from some other room or conveyed through apparatus that was faulty; laughter exploded in guffaws, or rippled, hardly heard.

'Thanks,' Father Clohessy said, reaching for the glass that had been filled for him.

There would be embarrassment if he mentioned the Church's slow collapse. There would be an awkwardness; best not said, his friends' opinion would be. Sometimes you had to close your mind down.

A sense of isolation, often creeping up on him during a Saturday evening in the Emmet Bar, did so again.

Centuries of devotion had created a way of life in which the mystery of the Trinity was taken for granted, the Church's invincible estate a part of every day, humility part of it, too, instead of rights plucked out of nowhere, order abandoned in favour of confusion. What priests and bishops had been – their strength and their parish people's salvation – was mocked in television farces, deplored, presented as absurdity. That other priests in other towns, in cities, in country parishes, were isolated by their celibacy, by the mourning black of their dress, had been a consolation once, but that source of comfort had long ago dried up.

The Offaly flags would be hoisted all right if Ger Toibin had been fit, his companions were agreeing. The final score was predicted; he joined in that, the talk went on. Houses were to be built on the Tinakilty road where the old cement works had been. Madden's Hotel would be closed for six months while improvements were put in. There were rumours of a fertilizer outfit taking over Williamson's Yard.

'Are you off so?' Father Clohessy heard himself asked when half an hour had passed, then heard it said that he would surely have another.

He shook his head, finishing his second cigarette and stubbing out the butt. There were a few more exchanges, before he pushed his way through the drinkers, his hand shaken once or twice, salutes of farewell.

In the darkening streets of the town his reverie

continued. A kind of truth it was, somewhere at the heart of his vocation, that there should be awareness of the holy world that was lost – yet he could not ever deny that vocation claimed its postulants as it wished. Companionable and easy, Father Finaghy led the sing-songs in the Emmet Bar on a Saturday evening, a little tipsy and none the worse for that.

Slowly, as Father Clohessy walked on, these well-worn reflections were left behind in the town that was half closed down for the night. Nothing replaced them for a while, before the careful hands of Justina Casey lifted down the altar ornaments, her polishing rags and Brasso pads tidily laid out. She touched away from a lily a petal that had gone brown. She scraped off the candle grease that had accumulated on the candle-holders. She re-arranged the missionary leaflets.

It was what there was; it was what he had, whether he understood it or not. Justina Casey would stay in the town because Mr Gilfoyle would make sure she didn't get on the Dublin bus; Maeve would keep an eye on her; after a time Breda Maguire would forget about her. In the confined space of the confessional there would again be the unnecessary confessions, again the granting of absolution. Then happiness would break in the face that saw God in his own.

An Evening Out

In the theatre bar they still talked, not hurrying over their drinks although an announcement had warned that the performance would begin in two minutes. There were more people in the bar than it could comfortably accommodate, crushed close against the bar itself and in the corners, some just beginning to make their way through the several doorways to the auditorium.

'The performance will begin in one minute,' the peremptory Tannoy voice reminded, and quite suddenly the bar was almost empty.

The barman was a character, gloomy-faced, skin and bone, bespectacled; lank like old string, he said himself. The barmaid was younger by quite a bit, and cheerfully plump.

'Oh, look,' she said. 'That woman.'

One woman had not left with the others and showed no sign of doing so. She was in a corner, sitting at one of the few tables the bar provided. All around her, on the shelf that ran around the walls, on the seats of chairs, there were empty glasses. Her own was three-quarters full of gin and tonic.

'Deaf, d'you think?' the barman wondered and the

barmaid remarked that the theatre was never a place for the hard of hearing, it stood to reason. It could be of course that a deaf-aid had been temporarily turned off and then forgotten.

The woman they spoke of was smartly dressed, two shades of green; a coat that was tweed on one side and waterproof on the other was draped over the other chair at her table. The remains of beauty strikingly lit her features, seeming to be there less casually, less incidentally, than beauty might have been earlier in her life. Touches of grey were allowed in her fair hair, adding a distinction that went with the other changes time had wrought.

'Excuse me, madam,' the barman said, 'but the performance has begun.'

★

What a city London is! Jeffrey thought, staring up at the dark bronze features of Sir Henry Havelock beneath the sprinkling of pigeon droppings that lightened the soldier's crown. The last of an April twilight was slipping away, the city at its best, as it also was – in Jeffrey's view – when dawn was turning into day. In Trafalgar Square the traffic was clogged, a crawl of lumbering red buses and patient taxis, a cyclist now and again weaving through. People gathered at the crossing lights, seeming to lose something of themselves in each small multitude while obediently they waited to move

forward when the signal came. Pigeons swooped above
territory they claimed as theirs, and landed on it to
waddle after tit-bits, or snapped at one another, flapping
away together into the sky, still in dispute.

Jeffrey turned away from it all, from Sir Henry
Havelock and the pigeons and the four great lions, the
floodlights just turned on, illuminating the façade of
the National Gallery. 'Won't do to keep her waiting,'
he murmured, causing two girls who were passing to
snigger. He kept her waiting longer, for when he
reached it he entered the Salisbury in St Martin's Lane
and ordered a Bell's, and then called out that it had
better be a double.

He needed it. Truth to tell, he needed a second but
he shook away the thought, reprimanding himself:
neither of them would get anywhere if he was tipsy.
On the street again he searched the pockets of his
mackintosh for the little plastic container that was
rattling somewhere, and when he found it in his jacket
he took two of his breath fresheners.

*

Evelyn drew back slightly from the barman's elderly,
untidy face, from cheeks that fell into hollows, false
teeth. He said again that the performance had begun.

'Thank you,' she said. 'Actually, I'm waiting for
someone.'

'We could send your friend in if you liked to go

on ahead. If you have your ticket. They're sometimes not particular about a disturbance before a play's got going.'

'No, actually we're just meeting here. We're not going to the theatre.'

She read, behind heavily rimmed lenses, bewilderment in the man's eyes. It was unusual, she read next, the thought flitting through his confusion. He settled for that, a conclusion reached.

'You didn't mind my asking? Only I said to my colleague where's the need for both of them to be late if they have their tickets on them?'

'It's very kind of you.'

'Thank you, madam.'

Near to where she sat he cleared the shelf of glasses, wiped it down with a damp grey cloth, moved on, expertly balancing the further glasses he collected. 'Lady's waiting for her friend,' he said to the barmaid, who was washing up at a sink behind the bar. 'They're not attending the show tonight.'

Evelyn was aware of the glances from behind the bar. Speculation would come later, understandable when there was time to kill. For the moment she was no more than a woman on her own.

'D'you think I could have another?' she called out, suddenly deciding to. 'When you have a minute?'

She speculated herself then, wondering about whoever was destined to walk in. Oh, Lord! she so often had thought when an unsuitable arrival had abruptly brought such wondering to an end. 'Oh no,' she had even murmured to herself, looking away in a futile pretence that she was expecting no one. Doggedly they had always come – the Lloyd's bank manager, the choral-music enthusiast, the retired naval officer who turned out to be a cabin steward, the widowed professor who had apologized and gone away, the one who made up board games. Even before they spoke, their doggedness and their smiles appeared to cover a multitude of sins.

She had all her life been obsessively early for appointments, and waiting yet again she made a resolution: this time if it was no good there wouldn't be a repetition. She'd just leave it; though of course a disappointment, it might be a relief.

Her drink came. The barman didn't linger. She shook her head when he said he'd bring her change.

'That's very kind of you, madam.'

She smiled that away, and was still smiling when a man appeared in the open doorway. He was hesitant, looking about him as if the place were crowded and there were several women to choose from, his nervousness not disguised. When he came closer he nodded before he spoke.

'Jeffrey,' he said. 'Evie?'

'Well, Evelyn actually.'

'Oh, I'm awfully sorry.'

His mackintosh was worn in places but wasn't grubby. His high cheekbones stood out, the skin tight where they stretched it. He didn't look at all well nourished. His dark hair, not a fleck of grey in it, was limp and she wondered if perhaps he was recovering from flu.

'Would you like your drink topped up?' he offered in a gentlemanly way. 'Nuts? Crisps?'

'No, I'm happy, thanks.'

He was fastidious, you could tell. Was there a certain vulnerability beneath that edgy manner? She always stipulated well-spoken and on that he could not be faulted. If he was recovering from even a cold, he'd naturally look peaky; no one could help that. He took off his mackintosh and a blue muffler, revealing a tweed jacket that almost matched the pale brown of his corduroy trousers.

'My choice of rendezvous surprise you?' he said.

'Perhaps a little.'

It didn't now that she had met him, for there was something about him that suggested he thought things out: theatre bars were empty places when a performance was on; there wouldn't be the embarrassment of approaches made by either of them to the wrong person. He didn't say that, but she knew. Belatedly he apologized for keeping her waiting.

'It doesn't matter in the least.'

'You're sure I can't bring you another drink?'

'No, really, thank you.'

'Well, I'll just get something for myself.'

★

At the bar Jeffrey asked about wine. 'D'you have white? Dry?'

'Indeed we do, sir.' The barman reached behind him and lifted a bottle from an ice bucket. 'Grinou,' he said. 'We like to keep it cool, being white.'

'Grinou?'

'It's what the wine's called, sir. La Combe de Grinou. The label's a bit washed away, but that's what it's called. Very popular in here, the Grinou is.'

Jeffrey took against the man, the way he often did with people serving him. He guessed that the barmaid looked after the man in a middle-aged daughterly way, listening to his elderly woes and ailments, occasionally inviting him to a Christmas celebration. Her daytime work was selling curtain material, Jeffrey surmised; the man had long ago retired from the same department store. Something like that it would be, the theatre bar their real world.

'All right, I'll try a glass,' he said.

*

They talked for a moment about the weather and then about the bar they were in, commenting on the destruction of its Georgian plasterwork, no more than a corner of the original ceiling remaining. From time to time applause or laughter reached them from the theatre's auditorium. Gingerly in their conversation they moved on to more personal matters.

Forty-seven they'd said he was. *Photographer* they'd given as his profession on the personal details' sheet, and she had thought of the photographers you saw on television, a scrum of them outside a celebrity's house or pushing in at the scene of a crime. But on the phone the girl had been reassuring: a newspaper photographer wasn't what was meant. 'No, not at all like that,' the girl had said. 'Nor weddings neither.' Distinguished in his field, the girl had said; there was a difference.

She tried to think of the names of great photographers and could remember only Cartier-Bresson, without a single image coming into her mind. She wondered about asking what kind of camera he liked best, but asked instead what kind of photographs he took.

'Townscapes,' he said. 'Really only townscapes.'

She nodded confidently, as if she caught the significance of that, as if she appreciated the attraction of photographing towns.

'Parts of Islington,' he said. 'Those little back streets in Hoxton. People don't see what's there.'

His lifetime's project was to photograph London in all its idiosyncrasies. He mentioned places: Hungerford Bridge, Drummond Street, Worship Street, Brick Lane, Wellclose Square. He spoke of manhole covers and shadows thrown by television dishes, and rain on slated roofs.

'How very interesting,' she said.

What she sought was companionship. Sometimes when she made her way to the Downs or the coast she

66

experienced the weight of solitude; often in the cinema or the theatre she would have liked to turn to someone else to say what she'd thought of this interpretation or that. She had no particular desire to be treated to candle-lit dinners, which the bureau – the Bryanston Square Introduction Bureau – had at first assumed would be a priority; but she would not have rejected such attentions, provided they came from an agreeable source. Marriage did not come into it, but nor was it entirely ruled out.

People she knew were not aware that she was a client at the Bryanston Square Bureau, not that she was ashamed of it. There would perhaps have been some surprise, but easily she could have weathered that. What was more difficult to come to terms with, and always had been, was the uneasy sense that the truth seemed to matter less than it should, both in the agency itself and in the encounters it provided. As honestly as she knew how, she had completed the personal details' sheet, carefully deliberating before she so much as marked, one way or the other, each little box, correctly recording her age, at present fifty-one; and when an encounter took place she was at pains not to allow mistaken impressions to go unchecked. But even so there was always that same uneasiness, the nagging awareness that falsity was natural in what she was engaged upon.

★

'You drive?' he asked.

He watched her nod, covering her surprise. It always took them aback, that question; he couldn't think why. She seemed quite capable, he thought, and tried to remember what it said on the information he'd been sent. Had she been involved with a language school? Something like that came back to him and he mentioned it.

'That was a while ago,' she said.

She was alone now; and, as Jeffrey understood it, devoted some of her time to charity work; he deduced that there must be private means.

'My mother died in nineteen ninety-seven,' she said. 'I looked after her during her last years. A full-time occupation.'

Jeffrey imagined a legacy after the mother's death; the father, he presumed, had departed long before.

'I'm afraid photography is something I don't know much about,' she said, and he shrugged, vaguely indicating that that was only to be expected. A tooth ached a bit, the same one as the other night and coming on as suddenly, the last one on the right, at the bottom.

'You found it interesting,' he said, 'languages and that?'

She was more promising than the insurance woman, or the hospital sister they'd tried so hard to interest him in. He'd said no to both, but they'd pressed, the way they sometimes did. He'd been indifferent this time, but even so he'd agreed. While he prodded cautiously with his tongue he learnt that passing on a familiarity with foreign languages was, in fact, not a particularly interesting way of making a living. He wondered if the barman kept aspirin handy; more likely, though, the barmaid might have some; or the Gents might run to a dispenser.

'Excuse me a sec,' he said.

'Oh yes, there's something in the Gents,' the old barman said when the barmaid had poked about in her handbag and had shaken her head. 'Just inside the door, sir.'

But when Jeffrey put a pound in nothing came out. Too late he saw – scrawled on a length of perforated stamp paper and stuck too high to be noticed – *Out of order*. He swore hotly. If the woman hadn't been there he'd have created a scene, demanding his pound back, even claiming he had put in two.

'You have a car?' he enquired quite bluntly when he returned to the theatre bar, because on the way back from the Gents it had occurred to him that she had only said she could drive. *Driver?* it enquired on the wretchedly long-winded personal data thing, but he always asked, just to be sure. He was modest in his expectations where the Bryanston Square Introduction Bureau was concerned. He sought no more than a car-owner who would transport him and his photographic equipment from one chosen area of London to another, someone who – as privately he put it to himself – would be drawn into his work. He imagined a quiet person, capable after instruction of unfolding and setting up a tripod, of using a simple light-meter, of making notes and keeping a record, who would enjoy becoming part of things. He imagined conversations that were all to do with the enterprise he had undertaken; nothing more was necessary. He naturally had not revealed any of these details on the Bryanston Square application form he had completed eighteen months ago, believing that it would be unwise to do so.

'It's just I wondered,' he said in the theatre bar, 'if you possessed a car?'

He watched her shaking her head. She'd had a car until a year ago, a Nissan. 'I hardly ever used it,' she explained. 'I really didn't.'

He didn't let his crossness show, but disappointment felt like a weight within him. It wearied him, as disappointment had a way of doing. The nearest there'd ever been was the social worker with the beaten-up Ford Escort, or ages before that the club receptionist with the Mini. But neither had lasted long enough to be of any real help and both had turned unpleasant in the end. All that wasted effort, this time again; he might as well just walk away, he thought.

'My turn to get us a drink,' she said, taking a purse from her handbag and causing him to wonder if she had an aspirin in there too.

He didn't ask. He'd thought as he set out that if yet again there was nothing doing there might at least be the consolation of dinner – which references to toothache could easily put the kibosh on. He wondered now about L'Etape. He'd often paused to examine the menu by the door.

'Wine, this was.' He handed her his glass and watched her crossing the empty space to the bar. She wasn't badly dressed: no reason why she shouldn't be up to L'Etape's tariff.

*

She listened while he went through his cameras, giving the manufacturers' names, and details about flash and exposure. Nine he had apparently, a few of them very old and better than any on the market now. His book about London had been commissioned and would run to almost a thousand pages.

'Gosh!' she murmured. Halfway through her third gin and tonic, she felt pleasantly warm, happy enough to be here, although she knew by now that none of this was any good. 'Heavens, you'll be busy!' she said. His world was very different from hers, she added, knowing she must not go on about hers, that it would be tedious to mention all sorts of things. Why should anyone be interested in her rejection more than twenty years ago of someone she had loved? Why should anyone be interested in knowing that she had done so, it seemed now, for no good reason beyond the shadow of doubt there'd been? A stranger would not see the face that she still saw, or hear the voice she heard; or understand why, afterwards, she had wanted no one else; or hear what, afterwards, had seemed to be a truth – that doubt played tricks in love's confusion. And who could expect a stranger to want to hear about the circumstances of a mother's lingering illness and the mercy of her death in a suburban house? You put it all together and it made a life; you lived in its aftermath, but that, too, was best kept back. She smiled at her companion through these reflections, for there was no reason not to.

'I was wondering about L'Etape,' he said.

Imagining this to be another camera, she shook her head, and he said that L'Etape was a restaurant. It was difficult then, difficult to say that perhaps they should not begin something that could not be continued, which his manner suggested had been his conclusion also. They were not each other's kind: what at first had seemed to be a possibility hadn't seemed so after three-quarters of an hour, as so often was the way. So much was right: she would have liked to say so; she would have liked to say that she'd enjoyed their encounter and hoped he'd shared that with her. Her glass was nowhere near empty, nor was his; there was no hurry.

'But then I'd best get back,' she said. 'If you don't mind.'

She wondered if in his life, too, there had been a mistake that threw a shadow, if that was why he was looking around for someone to fill a gap he had never become used to. She smiled in case her moment of curiosity showed, covering it safely over.

'It was just a thought,' he said. 'L'Etape.'

★

The interval curtain came down at an emotional moment. There was applause, and then the first chattering voices reached the bar, which filled up quickly. The noise of broken conversation spread in the quiet it had disturbed, until the Tannoy announcement warned that three minutes only remained, then two, and one.

'I'm afraid we shut up shop now,' the elderly barman said and the plump barmaid hurried about, collecting the glasses and pushing the chairs against one wall so that the cleaners could get at the floor when they came in the morning. 'Sorry about that,' the barman apologized.

Jeffrey considered making a fuss, insisting on another drink, since the place after all was a public bar. He imagined waking up at two or three in the morning and finding himself depressed because of the way the evening had gone. He would remember then the stern features of Sir Henry Havelock in Trafalgar Square and the two girls giggling because he'd said something out loud. He would remember the *Out of order* sign in the Gents. She should have been more explicit about the driving on that bloody form instead of wasting his time.

He thought of picking up a glass and throwing it at the upside-down bottles behind the bar, someone's leftover slice of lemon flying through the air, glass splintering into the ashtrays and the ice-bucket, all that extra for them to clear up afterwards. He thought of walking away without another word, leaving the woman to make her peace with the pair behind the bar. Ridiculous they were, ridiculous not to have an aspirin somewhere.

★

'It was brilliant, your theatre-bar idea,' she said as they passed through the foyer. The audience's laughter reached them, a single ripple, quietening at once. The box office was closed, a board propped up against its ornate brass bars. Outside, the posters for the play they hadn't seen wildly proclaimed its virtues.

'Well,' he said, though without finality; uncertain, as in other ways he had seemed to be.

Yet surely she hadn't been mistaken; surely he must have known also, and as soon as she had. She imagined him with one of his many cameras, skulking about the little streets of Hoxton. There was no reason why a photographer shouldn't have an artistic temperament, which would account for his nerviness or whatever it was.

'I don't suppose,' he said, 'you'd have an aspirin?'

He had a toothache. She searched her handbag, for she sometimes had paracetamol.

'I'm sorry,' she said, still rummaging.

'It doesn't matter.'

'It's bad?'

He said he would survive. 'I'll try the Gents in L'Etape. Sometimes there's a vending machine in a Gents.'

They fell into step. It wasn't why he'd suggested L'Etape, he said. 'It's just that I felt it would be nice,' he said. 'A regretful dinner.'

When they came to a corner, he pointed up a narrower, less crowded street than the one they'd walked along. 'It's there,' he said. 'That blue light.'

Feeling sorry for him, she changed her mind.

★

The hat-check girl brought paracetamol to their table, since there wasn't a vending machine in the Gents. Jeffrey thanked her, indicating with a gesture that he would tip her later. At a white grand piano a pianist in a plum-coloured jacket reached out occasionally for a concoction in a tall lemonade glass, not ceasing to play his Scott Joplin medley. A young French waiter brought menus and rolls. He made a recommendation but his English was incomprehensible. Jeffrey asked him to repeat what he'd said, but it was hopeless. Typical, that was, Jeffrey thought, ordering lamb, with peas and polenta.

'I'm sorry about your toothache,' she said.

'It'll go.'

The place was not quite full. Several tables, too close to the piano, were still unoccupied. Someone applauded when the pianist began a showy variation of 'Mountain Greenery'. He threw his head about as he played, blond hair flopping.

'Shall I order the wine?' Jeffrey offered. 'D'you mind?' He never said beforehand that he intended not to pay. Better just to let it happen, he always thought.

'No, of course I don't mind,' she said.

'That's kind of you.' He felt better than he had all evening, in spite of the nagging in his lower jaw and that, he knew, would lessen when the paracetamol got going. It was always much better when they said yes to a regretful dinner, when the disappointment began to slip away. 'We'll have the Lamothe Bergeron,' he ordered. 'The '95.'

*

She was aware that a woman at a distant table, in a corner where there were potted plants, kept glancing at her. The woman was with two men and another woman. She seemed faintly familiar; so did one of the men.

'*Madame,*' the young waiter interrupted her efforts to place the couple, arriving with the escalope she'd ordered. '*Bon appétit, madame.*'

'Thank you.'

She liked the restaurant, the thirties' style, the pale blue lighting, the white grand piano, the aproned waiters. She liked her escalope when she tasted it, and the heavily buttered spinach, the little out-of-season new potatoes. She liked the wine.

'Not bad, this place,' her companion said. 'What d'you think?'

'It's lovely.'

They talked more easily than they had in the theatre bar and it was the theatre bar they spoke about, since it was their common ground. Odd, they'd agreed, that old barman had been; odd, too, that 'barmaid' should still be a common expression, implying in this case someone much younger, the word hanging on from another age.

'Oh, really . . .' she began when a second bottle of wine was suggested, and then she thought why not? They talked about the Bryanston Square Bureau, which was common ground too.

'They muddle things up,' he said. 'They muddle people up. They get them wrong, with all their little boxes and their questionnaires.'

'Yes, perhaps they do.'

The woman who'd kept glancing across the restaurant was listening to one of the men, who appeared to be telling a story. There was laughter when he finished. The second man lit a cigarette.

'Heavens!' Evelyn exclaimed, although she hadn't meant to.

★

Jeffrey turned to look and saw, several tables away, four smartly dressed people, one of the two women in a striped black and scarlet dress, the other with glasses, her pale blonde hair piled elaborately high. The men were darkly suited. Like people in an advertisement, he thought, an impression heightened by the greenery that was a background to their table. He knew the kind.

'They're friends of yours?' he asked.

'The woman in red and the man who's smoking have the flat above mine.'

She'd sold some house or other, he heard; a family house, it then became clear. She'd sold it when her mother died and had bought instead the flat she spoke of, more suitable really for a person on her own. Pasmore the people she had suddenly recognized were called. She didn't know them.

'But they know you, eh?'

He felt quite genial; the diversion passed the time.

'They've seen me,' she said.

'Coming and going, eh?'

'That kind of thing.'

'Coffee? Shall we have coffee?'

He signalled for a waiter. He would go when the wine was finished; usually he went then, slipping off to the Gents, then picking up his coat. Once there had been a complaint to the bureau about that but he'd said the woman had invited him to dinner – Belucci's it was that time – and had become drunk before the evening finished, forgetting what the arrangement had been.

'I'll hold the fort,' he said, 'if you want to say hullo to your friends.'

She smiled and shook her head. He poured himself more wine. He calculated that there were four more glasses left in the bottle and he could tell she'd had enough. The coffee came and she poured it, still smiling at him in a way he found bewildering. He calculated the amount she'd had to drink: two gin and tonics he'd counted earlier, and now the wine, a good four glasses. 'I wouldn't even know the Pasmores' name,' she was saying, 'except that it's on their bell at the downstairs door.'

He moved the wine bottle in case she reached out for it. The pianist, silent for a while, struck up again, snatches from *West Side Story*.

'It's lovely here,' she murmured, and Jeffrey would have sworn her eyes searched for his. He felt uneasy, his euphoria of a few moments ago slipping away; he hoped there wasn't going to be trouble. In an effort to distract her mood, he said:

'Personally, I shan't be bothering the Bryanston Square Bureau again.'

She didn't appear to hear, although that wasn't surprising in the din that was coming from the piano.

'I don't suppose,' she said, 'you have a cigarette about you?'

Her smile, lavish now, had spread into all her features. She'd ticked *Non-smoker* on the information sheet, she said, but all that didn't really matter any more. He pressed a thumbnail along the edge of the transparent cover of the Silk Cut packet he had bought in the Salisbury and held it out to her across the table.

'I used to once,' she said. 'When smoking was acceptable.'

She took a cigarette and he picked up a little box of matches with *L'Etape* on it. He struck one for her, her fingers touching his. He lit a cigarette for himself.

'How good that is!' She blew out smoke, leaning forward as she spoke, cheeks flushed, threads of smoke drifting in the air. 'I used to love a cigarette.'

She reached a hand out as if to seize one of his, but played instead with the salt-cellar, pushing it about. She was definitely tiddly. With her other hand she held her cigarette in the air, lightly between two fingers, as Bette Davis used to in her heyday.

'It's a pity you sold your car,' he said, again seeking a distraction.

She didn't answer that, but laughed, as if he'd been amusing, as if he'd said something totally different. She was hanging on his words, or so it must have seemed to the people who had recognized her, so intent was her scrutiny of his face. She'll paw me, Jeffrey thought, before the evening's out.

'They're gathering up their things,' she said. 'They're going now.'

He didn't turn around to see, but within a minute or so the people passed quite close. They smiled at her, at Jeffrey too. Mr Pasmore inclined his head; his wife gave a little wave with her fingers. They would gossip about this to the residents of the other flats if they considered it worthwhile to do so: the solitary woman in the flat below theirs had something going with a younger man. No emotion stirred in Jeffrey, neither sympathy nor pity, for he was not given to such feelings. A few drinks and a temptation succumbed to, since temptation wasn't often there: the debris of all that was nothing much when the audience had gone, and it didn't surprise him that it was simply left there, without a comment.

When a waiter came, apologetically to remind them that they were at a table in the no-smoking area, she stubbed her cigarette out. Her features settled into composure; the flush that had crept into her cheeks drained away. A silence gathered while this normality returned and it was she in the end who broke it, as calmly as if nothing untoward had occurred.

'Why did you ask me twice if I possessed a car?'

'I thought I had misunderstood.'

'Why did it matter?'

'Someone with a car would be useful to me in my work. My gear is heavy. I have no transport myself.'

He didn't know why he said that; he never had before. In response her nod was casual, as if only politeness had inspired the question she'd asked. She nodded again when he said, not knowing why he said it either:

'Might our dinner be your treat? I'm afraid I can't pay.'

She reached across the table for the bill the waiter had brought him. In silence she wrote a cheque and asked him how much she should add on.

'Oh, ten per cent or so.'

She took a pound from her purse, which Jeffrey knew was for the hat-check girl.

★

They walked together to an Underground station. The townscapes were a weekend thing, he said: he photographed cooked food to make a living. Hearing which tins of soup and vegetables his work appeared on, she wondered if he would add that his book of London would never be completed, much less published. He didn't, but she had guessed it anyway.

'Well, I go this way,' he said when they had bought their tickets and were at the bottom of the escalators.

He'd told her about the photographs he was

ashamed of because she didn't matter; without resentment she realized that. And witnessing her excursion into foolishness, he had not mattered either.

'Your toothache?' she enquired and he said it had gone.

They did not shake hands or remark in any way upon the evening they'd spent together, but when they parted there was a modest surprise: that they'd made use of one another was a dignity compared with what should have been. That feeling was still there while they waited on two different platforms and while their trains arrived and drew away again. It lingered while they were carried through the flickering dark, as intimate as a pleasure shared.

Graillis's Legacy

He hadn't meant to break his journey but there was time because he was early, so Graillis made a detour, returning to a house he hadn't visited for twenty-three years. A few miles out on the Old Fort road, devoured by rust, the entrance gates had sagged into undergrowth. The avenue was short, twisting off to the left, the house itself lost behind a line of willows.

When the woman who'd been left a widow in it had sold up and gone to Dublin, a farmer acquired the place for its mantelpieces and the lead of its roof. He hadn't ever lived there, but his car had been drawn up on the gravel when the house was first empty and Graillis had gone back, just once. Since then there'd been talk of everything falling into disrepair, not that there hadn't been signs of this before, the paint of the windows flaking, the garden neglected. The woman on her own hadn't bothered much; although it had never otherwise been his nature to do so, her husband had seen to everything.

Graillis didn't get out of his car, instead turned it slowly on the grass that had begun to grow through the gravel. He drove away, cautious on the pot-holed surface of the avenue, then slowed by the bends of a narrow side-road. A further mile on, a signpost guided him to the town he had chosen for his afternoon's business. An hour's drive from the town he lived in himself, it was more suitable for his purpose because he wasn't known there.

Still with time to spare, he parked and took a ticket from a machine. He locked his car and went to look for Davitt Street, where he enquired in a newsagent's and was told that Lenehan and Clifferty's office was four doors further on, what used to be the old Co-op Hardware.

'Mr Clifferty won't keep you a minute,' the girl assured him in the spacious reception area where the day's newspapers were laid out. Only last week's *Irish Field* had been unfolded.

'You were recommended to us, Mr Graillis?' Clifferty asked, having apologized because there'd been a wait of much longer than a minute. He was a man in a tweed suit, with a tie of the same material, and garnet cufflinks. He was stylish for a country solicitor, his considerable bulk crowned by a full head of prematurely white hair. Graillis was less at ease in comparison, more humbly attired in corduroy trousers and an imitation suede jacket. He was an angular, thin man of fifty-nine, his fair hair receding and touched with grey.

'You're in the Golden Pages,' he responded to the solicitor's query.

He passed the envelope he'd brought with him

across the green leather surface of a tidy desk that was embossed with a pattern at the corners. Clifferty extracted a folded sheet of writing paper and when he'd read its contents made a single note on a pad, then read the letter again.

'She was a woman a while back,' Graillis said.

'Well, if I've got this right, you're not attempting anything illegal, Mr Graillis. A legacy can be rejected.'

'It's that I was wondering about.'

Clifferty returned the letter to its envelope but didn't hand it back. 'These people are a reputable firm of solicitors. We do some business with them. I can write to say the inheritance is an embarrassment if that's what you'd like me to do. The estate would be wound up in the usual way, with the proposed bequest left in as part of it.'

'I wouldn't want to turn my back on the thought that was there. Since I'm mentioned in the will I wouldn't want to do that.'

'You're more than mentioned, Mr Graillis. From what's indicated in the notification you received, no one much else is. Besides charities.'

Sensing the content of the solicitor's thoughts, Graillis was aware of an instinct to contradict them. It was understandable that the interest of a country solicitor should be fed by what he assumed, that the routine of family law in a provincial town should make room for a hint of the dramatic. Graillis might have supplied the facts, but did not do so.

'Maybe some small memento,' he said. 'Maybe an ornament or a piece of china. Anything like that.'

'You've been left a sum of money that's not inconsiderable, Mr Graillis.'

'That's why I drove over, though – to see could I accept a little thing instead.'

There'd been an ashtray with a goldfinch on it, but in case it had since been broken, he didn't like to mention it. And there were dinner plates he'd always liked particularly, with a flowery edging in two shades of blue.

'Just something, was what I thought. If it would be possible.'

When the snowdrops spread in clumps beneath the trees, she'd said he might like some and would have given him what she had picked already. Wrapped in damp newspaper, they would keep their freshness, she said, and he tried to remember how it was she broke off what she was saying when she realized her suggestion wasn't possible. She had tried to settle the stems back in the water of the vase she'd taken them from but it was difficult, and then the floor was scattered with flowers gone limp already. It didn't matter, she could pick some more, she said.

'Oh, it would be possible, I'm sure,' Clifferty said, 'to have what you want. I only mention the other.'

The solicitor had a way of smoothing the wiry, reddish thicket of his eyebrows, a leisurely attention given first to one and then the other. He allowed himself this now, before he continued:

'But I should tell you I would require a sight of the will before advising you on any part of it.'

'Would they send it down from Dublin?'

'They'd send a copy.'

Clifferty nodded saying that, the conversation over. He asked Graillis what line he was in and Graillis said he was in charge of the branch library in the town where he lived. He added that a long time ago he had been employed in the Munster and Leinster Bank there, in the days when the bank was still called that. He stood up.

'Make an appointment with the girl outside for this day week, Mr Graillis,' Clifferty said before they shook hands.

*

He drove slowly through flat, unchanging landscape and stopped when he had almost reached the town he was returning to. No other car was drawn up outside the Jack Doyle Inn, no bicycle leant against the silver-painted two-bar railings that protected its windows. Inside, the woman who served him called him by his name.

She went away when, pouring him a John Jameson, she'd asked him how he was these days. 'Give a rap on the counter if you'll want something more,' she said, a smell of simmering bacon beginning to waft in from the cooking she returned to. There was no one else in the bar.

He should have explained to the solicitor that he was a widower, that there was no marriage now to be damaged by a legacy that might seem to indicate a deception in the past. He should have explained that his doubts about accepting so much, and travelling to seek advice in another town, had only to do with avoiding curiosity and gossip in his own. He didn't know why he hadn't explained, why it hadn't occurred to him that Clifferty had probably taken it upon himself to pity a wronged wife who was now being wronged again, that subterfuge and concealment were again being called upon.

He took his whiskey to a corner. It would not have seemed unusual to speak about his marriage, about love's transformation within it, about his grief when it was no longer there, about the moments and occasions it had since become. Caught in the drift of memory, he saw – as vividly as if it were still the time when love began – a girl in a convent uniform, green and blue, shyness in her bright, fresh face. Half smiling, she turned her head away, made to blush by her friends when the gawky junior from the Munster and Leinster Bank went by on the street. And she was shy again when, grown up, she walked for the first time into the bank with her father's weekly cheques and takings. In her middle age, the mother she had twice become made her only a little different, made her the person she remained until there was the tragedy of a winter's night, on an icy road three years ago.

Graillis sipped his whiskey and lit a cigarette and slowly smoked, then drank some more. Beneath his professional rectitude, the solicitor would naturally have been more interested in the woman of the legacy than in the wife. *In her sixty-eighth year* was the only tit-bit the letter he'd been given to read revealed: she'd been an older woman, he would have realized.

The whiskey warmed Graillis, the cigarette was a comfort. He hadn't explained because you couldn't explain, because there was too little to explain, not too much. But even so he might have said he was a widower. He sat a little longer, eyeing an ornamental sign near the door – white letters on blue enamel – *You May Telephone From Here*. 'A small one,' he said when his rapping on the surface of the counter brought a sleek-haired youth he remembered as a child. The girl in Lenehan and Clifferty's reception had given him a card with his next week's appointment noted on it, and the telephone number of Lenehan and Clifferty as well. It wasn't too late, a few minutes past five.

'If it's possible,' he said when the same girl answered. 'Just something I forgot to say to Mr Clifferty.'

Waiting, he lit another cigarette. His glass was on a shelf in front of him, beside an ashtray with *Coca-Cola* on it. 'Mr Clifferty?' he said when Clifferty said hullo.

'Good evening, Mr Graillis.'

'It's just I wanted to clear up a detail.'

'What detail's that, Mr Graillis?'

'I don't think I explained that I'm widowed.'

The solicitor made a sympathetic sound. Then he said he was sorry, and Graillis said:

'It's just if you thought my wife's alive it would have been misleading.'

'I follow what you're saying to me.'

'I didn't want a misunderstanding.'

'No.'

'It's difficult, a thing like this coming out of the blue.'

'I appreciate that, Mr Graillis, and I have your instruction. I'm sanguine it can be met. If there's anything else, if there's a worry at all, bring it with you when you come over next week.'

'It's only I wanted you to know what I told you just now. There's nothing else.'

'We'll say goodbye so.'

'Who'd get what I'm handing back?'

'Whoever's in line for it. Some grand-nephew somewhere, I'd hazard. There's often a grand-nephew.'

'Thanks,' Graillis said and, not knowing what else to do, returned the receiver to its hook.

He picked up his glass and took it back to the table he'd been sitting at. He had thought he would feel all right after he'd seen a solicitor, and had thought so again when the telephone sign had given him the idea of ringing up. But still there was the unease that had begun when the letter about the legacy came. He didn't know why he'd gone to the house; he didn't know why he'd got into a state because he hadn't told a man who was a stranger to him that he was widowed. It had been the whiskey talking when he'd said he wanted to clear up a detail; it was whiskey courage that had allowed him to dial the number. He was bewildered by the resurrection of a guilt that long ago had softened away to nothing. In that other time no pain had been caused, no hurt; he had managed the distortions that created falsity, the lies of silence; what he had been forgiven for was not seeming to be himself for a while. A crudity still remained in the solicitor's reading of the loose ends that still were there: the wronged wife haunting restlessly from her grave, the older woman claiming from hers the lover who had slipped away from her.

*

'God, we never had it worse!'

'Oh, we will, boy, we will.'

Deploring the fall in sheep prices, two men settled themselves at the bar. The sleek-haired youth returned to serve them, and then an older man came in, with a white greyhound on a leash. The youth poured Smithwick's for him and said the *Evening Herald* hadn't been dropped off the bus yet. 'Shocking,' the old man grumbled, hunching himself over the *Tullamore Tribune* instead.

Graillis finished what was left of his whiskey. After the accident, when the notice had appeared in the obituary columns of the *Irish Times*, no lines of condolence had come from the woman whose half-ruined house he had visited. He had thought there might be a note and then had thought it was not appropriate that there should be. She would have thought so too.

He stubbed out his second cigarette. He never smoked at home, continuing not to after he'd found himself alone there, and smoking was forbidden in the branch library, a restriction he insisted upon himself. But in the drawing-room he had sat in so often in the autumn of 1979 and during the winter and spring that followed it, a friendship had developed over cigarettes, touches of lipstick on the cork tips that had accumulated in the ashtray with the goldfinch on it. That settled in his thoughts, still as a photograph, arrested with a clarity that today felt cruel.

He carried his glass back to the bar. He talked for a moment about the weather to the sleek-haired youth before he left. 'Take care, Mr Graillis,' the boy called after him, and he said he would.

Driving on, he tried to think of nothing, not of the girl who had become his wife when he was still a junior in the Munster and Leinster Bank, not of the woman he'd got to know when she borrowed novels from his branch library. The landscape he passed through was much the same as the landscape had been before he'd called in at the public house. It didn't change when a sign in Irish and English indicated the town ahead, only doing so when the town's outskirts began: the first few bungalows, summer blossom in their trim gardens.

Cars with prices on their windscreens crowded Riordan's forecourt, *Your Nissan Dealer* a reminder of the franchise. He passed the electricity works and then the rusty green Raleigh sign, the two figures and their bicycles only there in places.

Evening traffic slowed his progress on the town's main street. He wound down the window beside him and rested his elbow on it. He had intended to go straight to where he lived but changed his mind and instead turned into Cartmill Street, where the branch library was. No traffic disturbed the quiet here. Sometimes boys rattled up and down on their skate-boards, but there were no boys now, and hardly a pedestrian. He parked beneath the lime trees where the walk by the river began and crossed the street to a small building crouched low among the abandoned warehouses that ran the length of Cartmill Street and gave it character, as the lime trees and the river did.

Today he had closed the library at one o'clock, the only weekday it was shut in the afternoon, when some of the main-street shops were also. He turned a key in the deadlock, another in the Yale, then pushed the pale-blue door open. It was a Mr Haverty – failed grocer of Lower North Street, lifelong bachelor, aficionado of Zane Grey among Wild West storytellers – who had nagged the county library service into letting the town have a branch library, who had become, in fact, its first librarian. Since those early days, when he was a borrower himself, Graillis had felt at home in these modest premises, the walls entirely shelves, a narrow counter near the door. He had been the branch library's most frequent visitor then, and when galloping arthritis made Mr Haverty's duties increasingly a burden it was Mr Haverty who nominated him as his successor, enticing him away from the superior prospects of the bank. And Graillis said yes before he had a chance to dwell on all the disadvantages. 'But why on earth?' the girl he'd married cried out in bewilderment and disappointment. His safe employment had been taken for granted; in time promotion would mean occupancy of a squat grey landmark in the town, the house above the bank, with railings and a grained hall door. She had married into that; books had never been an interest they shared, had never been, for her, a need.

The woman for whom they were had often been noticed by Graillis about the town, coming out of a shop, getting into her car, not the kind of woman he would ever have known. Tall, and beautiful in her way, there was a difference about her, suggested by her composure and her clothes, and she seemed more different still when vaguely she wondered where Mr Haverty was, not knowing he had retired. She smiled when they talked then, and Graillis hadn't seen her smile before. The next time they talked for longer, and after that more easily. When she asked him which novelists he recommended he introduced her to Proust and Malcolm Lowry, to Forster and Madox Ford, and Mrs Gaskell and Wilkie Collins. He got in another copy of *Dubliners* for her because the existing copy had been left out in the rain and rendered unintelligible. He drew her attention to *Brighton Rock* and *Tender is the Night*. She found Elizabeth Bowen for herself.

In her tidy drawing-room he poured the wine at lunchtime. Not feeling careless themselves, for they were not, they talked about the careless people of Scott Fitzgerald, about the Palace Flophouse, and Hangover Square and Dorlcote Mill. The struggles of Jude acquired new small dimensions, the goodness of Joe Gargery marked a day, as Mrs Proudie did and Daisy Miller. Ellen Wedgeworth died, Dermot Trellis slept. Maurice Bendrix embraced the wife of his friend.

They did not go in for telling one another the story of their lives. Their conversation was not like that, yet almost without their knowing it their lives were there, in a room made different by their friendship. They did not touch upon emotions, nor touch upon regret or anything that might have been; they did not lose control of words. They did not betray, she her finished past, he what still was there. She brought in coffee, he turned from gazing out at rain or cold spring sunshine, they spoke again of Wildfell Hall. Her front door wide behind her, she stood on the steps, and was there in his driving-mirror until the willow trees were there instead.

There was the beginning of gossip: his car seen on that road, people noticing that she came often to the library. It was not much but would become so; he knew that and so did she; they did not say it. When the days began to lengthen there had been three seasons. In summer they would sit outside, at the white table on the lawn, but summer did not come.

Graillis replaced on the shelves what had been returned earlier today, *The Garden of Allah* still read by someone, crime stories more popular, Georgette Heyer holding her own. Sunburnt spines enclosed a world that the smell of old paper made what it was. She had said she envied him this place.

He looked about him before he left. A poster hung from the counter by the door, advertising the Strawberry Festival in June. Above the door, in straw, there was St Brigid's Cross. It was on the evening of the day the removal vans had clattered empty through the town and later lumbered away full of her possessions that she'd said she envied him. They'd had to wait until *Seven Pillars of Wisdom* was stamped for Mrs Garraher before they said goodbye, a Tuesday it had been.

He locked the door behind him and drove away.

*

Hearts were forming in the lettuces of his vegetable beds. He cut one, and chives and parsley. He walked about before he collected what he'd left on the path that ran beside his vegetables, adding a tomato that had ripened beneath a cloche. He had never become used to the emptiness of this return to his garden and his house, and he supposed he never would. In his kitchen he opened tins of soup and sardines. He washed the lettuce.

'He phoned me afterwards,' he imagined Clifferty saying now, standing in a kitchen doorway, going through his day, his solicitor's caution estimating how much he could pass on. 'I don't know what that man's trouble was,' Clifferty said, and added that there hadn't been much else today.

There was whiskey somewhere; Graillis looked for it and found it among the kitchen bottles. He poured a little, mixed oil and vinegar for his salad. On the radio there was agricultural news, the latest from the markets, and then a brash disc-jockey pumped out his chatter before a cacophony began. Silence was a pleasure after that.

Laying out a knife and fork on the kitchen table, Graillis wondered if either of his children would phone tonight. There was no reason why one of them should. There'd been nothing wrong, no cause for concern, when he'd heard from both of them not long ago. He poured more whiskey, not wanting to eat yet. He couldn't remember any other time when he'd drunk alone in this house. He kept the whiskey for people who dropped in.

Taking his glass with him, he walked about his garden, among penstemons and roses and crocosmia not yet in bud. The row of artichokes he'd planted in

February stood as high as empty sunflowers. Lavender scented the warm twilight.

The whiskey talk was private now, a whisper from his orderly remembering that no longer nurtured panic. In visiting the solicitor, in going to the house, he had touched what should not be touched except in memory, where everything was there for ever and nothing could be changed. Retirement from a branch library would not bring much and so there'd been a gesture. A stranger's interpretation of that – what curiosity hatched or gossip spun – was neither here nor there. Again, instead, there was the fresh, bright face, the gentle shyness. Again, instead, the older woman lifted to her lips a tan-tipped cigarette touched with crimson. Again there was the happiness of marriage, again embraces were imagined.

There was no more, nor would there be. Not even an ornament, for that would cheat reality. Not even a piece of china, and he would write to say so. The winter flowers lay scattered in the shadow of a secret, deception honouring a silent love.

Solitude

I reach the lock by standing on the hall chair. I open the hall door and pull the chair back to the alcove. I comb my hair in the hallstand glass. I am seven years old, waiting for my father to come downstairs.

Our house is a narrow house with a blue hall door, in a square, in London. My father has been away and now he is back. *The first morning we'll go to the café.* Ages ago my mother read what he had written for me on the postcard. 'They're called the Pyramids,' she said when I pointed at the picture. And then: 'Not long before he's back.' But it was fifty days.

I hear him whistling on the stairs, 'London Bridge Is Falling Down', and then he hugs me, because he has come in the night when I was asleep. He doesn't believe it, he says, how I have grown. 'I missed you terribly,' he says.

We walk together, across the square to where the traffic and the streets are. 'Coffee,' my father says in the café. 'Coffee, please, and a slice of Russian cake for you-know-who.'

But all the time there is what happened and all the time I know I mustn't say. A child to witness such a thing was best forgotten, Mrs Upsilla said, and Charles nodded his long black head. No blame, Charles said; any child would play her games behind a sofa; all they'd had to do was look. 'No skin off my nose,' Charles said. 'No business of a poor black man's.' And not knowing I was still outside the kitchen door, Mrs Upsilla said it made her sick to her bones. Well, it was something, Charles reminded her, that my mother wouldn't take her friend to the bedroom that was my father's too. At least there was the delicacy of that. But Mrs Upsilla said what delicacy, and called my mother's friend a low-down man.

'You're learning French now?' my father says in the café. 'Do you like French?'

'Not as much as history.'

'What have you learnt in history?'

'That William the Conqueror's son also got an arrow in his eye.'

'Which eye? Did they say which eye?'

'No, I don't think so.'

In the café the waitress is the one who always comes to us. My father says that is because we always sit at the same table. He says our waitress has Titian hair; he says that's what that colour is. My father is always commenting on people, saying they have this or that, guessing about them, or asking questions. Often he falls into conversation with people who enquire the way on the street, and beggars, anyone who stops him, anyone in shops. 'Rich as a candy king,' I heard someone in the café say once, and my father laughed, shaking his head.

All the time in the café I want to tell him, because I tell him everything when he comes back from a journey. I want to tell him about the dream I had that same night, all of it happening again. 'Oh, horrid nightmare,' my mother comforted me, not knowing what it was about because I didn't say, because I didn't want to.

'The picture gallery?' my father suggests when we have had our coffee. 'Or the dolls' museum today? Look, I have this.'

He spreads out on the table a handkerchief he has bought, all faded colours, so flimsy you can see through it in places. Old, he says, Egyptian silk. There is a pattern and he draws his forefinger through it so that I can see it too. 'For you,' he says. 'For you.'

In the bus, on the way to the dolls' museum he talks about Egypt. So hot it could make your skin peel off, so hot you have to lie down in the afternoon. One day he'll bring me with him; one day he'll show me the Pyramids. He takes my hand when we walk the last bit.

I know the way, but when we get there the doll I like best isn't on her shelf. Unwell, the man says, getting better in hospital. It's his way of putting it, my father says. He asks the man: that doll, the Spanish doll, will be back next week. 'Well, we can come again,' my father promises. 'Who's going to stay up for the party?' he says when we're back in the house.

The party is tonight. In the kitchen the wine bottles are laid out, two long rows all the length of the table, and other bottles on trays, and glasses waiting to be filled. Charles comes specially early to help when there is a party. There always is when my father returns.

'You sit down there and have your sandwich.' Mrs Upsilla's grey head is bent over what she's cooking; she's too busy to look up. Charles winks at me and I try to wink back but I can't do it properly. He passes close to where I'm sitting and then the sandwich I don't want isn't there any more. 'Oh, there's a good girl,' Mrs Upsilla says when she asks if I've eaten it and I say yes. And Charles smiles. And Davie giggles and Abigail does.

Abigail and Davie aren't real, but most of the time they're there. They were that day, when the door opened and my mother and her friend came into the drawing-room. 'It's all right,' my mother said. 'She's not here.' And Davie giggled and Abigail did too and I made them be quiet.

'My, my,' Charles says in the kitchen when Mrs Upsilla calls me a good girl. He says it so often it annoys Mrs Upsilla. 'Why's he saying that?' she asks me every time. 'What's he on about?' And Charles always laughs.

I thank Mrs Upsilla for the sandwich I haven't eaten because she likes me to thank her for things. On the way upstairs I remember that when the person in the café said as rich as a candy king I heard my father repeating that to my mother afterwards; he said that maybe what the person meant was he was rich to have so beautiful a wife. Or you could take it differently,

Mrs Upsilla said when I told her: the person in the café could have been referring to my mother's inheritance.

Upstairs, my father is standing at the door of their bedroom, my mother is tidying the bed. He has brought her a handkerchief too, bigger than mine, and already she wears it as a scarf. 'So beautiful you are!' my father says and my mother laughs, a sound that's like the tinkling of a necklace he gave her once. The bath taps are dribbling in the bathroom, turned low for my mother's bath. 'Who's going to help me take the corks out?' my father says, and my mother asks him to open the window at the top. Her lips are soft when she kisses my forehead, her scent makes me want to close my eyes and always be able to smell it. 'Good darling,' she whispers.

In the kitchen my father draws out the corks and I make a pile of them, and count them. The red bottles are really green, he says, but you can't see that until they're empty. He cuts away the shiny covering over each cork before he puts the corkscrew in. 'Well, that's all done,' he says and asks how many and I say thirty-six. 'You take me to the picture gallery next time?' he says, and the dancing ladies come into my head, and the storm at the cricket match, and Saint Catherine, and the portrait of the artist. 'That to look forward to,' my father says before he goes upstairs again.

We play a game in my room, Abigail and Davie and I. We pretend we are in Egypt, climbing up a pyramid, and Abigail says we should be wearing our cotton sun hats because the sun can burn your head even through your hair. So we go down for them but then it's cooler so we walk about the streets. We buy things in a market, presents to bring home, rings and brooches and jars of Egyptian peaches, and Egyptian chocolate and Egyptian rugs for the floor. Then I go back to the kitchen.

Charles has gone out for ice. 'You going to keep me company?' Mrs Upsilla says, still busy with her cooking. 'You'll trip on those laces,' she says, allowing the electric mixer to operate on its own for a moment. A nasty accident there could be, and she ties my laces. Always double-tie a shoelace, she says, and I go away.

In the drawing-room the bowls of olives and tit-bits are laid out; the fire is blazing, the wire net of the fire-guard drawn down. I watch the raindrops sliding on the window-panes. I watch the people in the square, hurrying through the rain, a woman holding an umbrella over her dog, Charles returning with the ice. The cars go slowly, the street lights have come on.

I sit in the armchair by the fire, looking at the pictures in the books, the old woman who kept children in a cage, the giants, the dwarfs, the Queen's reflection in the looking-glass. I look out into the square again: my mother's friend is the first to come. He waits for a car to pass before he crosses the square, and then there is the doorbell and his footsteps on the stairs.

'Have one of these,' he says in the drawing-room: cheese straws that Mrs Upsilla has made. 'Time for your dancing lesson,' and he puts the music on. He shows me the same steps again because I never try, because I don't want to try. 'How are they?' he asks and I know he means Davie and Abigail; ever since my mother mentioned them to him he asks about them. I might have told him they were there that afternoon, but instead I just say they're all right. Then other people come and he talks to them. I hate him so much I wish he could be dead.

I listen from one of the window-seats, half behind the curtain. A man is telling about a motor race he has taken part in. One of these days he'll win, a woman says. In his white jacket, Charles offers the drinks.

Other people come. 'Well, goodness me!' Mr Fairlie smiles down at me, and then he sits beside me. Old and tired, he says, not up to this gallivanting. He asks me what I did today and I tell him about the dolls' museum. He manages on his own, Mrs Upsilla told me, since his wife died. My mother went to the funeral, but he doesn't talk about that now. 'Poor old boy,' Charles said.

You can hardly hear the music because so many people are talking. Every time Charles passes by with another tray he waves to me with a finger and Mr Fairlie says that's clever. 'Well, look at you two!' a woman says and she kisses Mr Fairlie and kisses me, and then my father comes. 'Who's sleepy?' he says and he takes me from the party.

It will be ages before he goes away again: he promises

that before he turns the light out, but in the dark it's like it was in the dream. He'll go away and he won't come back, not ever wanting to. There'll never be the picture gallery again, our favourite picture the picnic on the beach. There'll never be the café again, there'll never be the dolls' museum. He'll never say, 'Who's sleepy?'

In the dark I don't cry although I want to. I make myself think of something else, of the day there was an accident in the square, of the day a man came to the door, thinking someone else lived in our house. And then I think about Mr Fairlie on his own. I see him as clearly as I did when he was beside me on the window-seat, the big freckles on his forehead, his wisps of white hair, his eyes that don't look old at all. 'A surgeon in his day,' Mrs Upsilla told Charles the morning my mother went to the funeral. I see Mr Fairlie in his house although I've never been there. I see him cooking for himself as best he can, and with a Hoover on the stairs. 'Who'd mind being cut up by Mr Fairlie?' Charles said once.

The music's so faint it sounds as if it's somewhere else, not in our house, and I wonder if they're dancing. By ten o'clock the party will be over, Mrs Upsilla said, and then they'll go off to different restaurants, or maybe they'll all go to the same one, and some will just go home. It's that kind of party, not lasting for very long, not like some Mrs Upsilla has known. 'Here?' Charles asked, surprised when she said that. 'Here in this house?' And she said no, not ever an all-night party here, and Charles nodded in his solemn way and said you'd know it. He'll stay for an hour or so when everyone has gone, helping Mrs Upsilla to clear up. I've never been awake then.

Davie says it was some kind of game. Fun, he says, but Abigail shakes her head, her black plaits flying about. I don't want to talk about it. A Wednesday it was, Mrs Upsilla gone off for the afternoon, Charles tending the flowerbeds in the square.

I try to think about Mr Fairlie again, having to make his bed, doing all the other things his wife did, but Mr Fairlie keeps slipping away. My mother's dress was crumpled on the floor and I could see it when I peeped out, her necklace thrown down too. Afterwards, she said they should have locked the door.

The music is still far away. The noise of the people isn't like people talking, more like a hum. I push the bedclothes back and tip-toe to the stairs to look down through the banisters. Mrs Upsilla is dressed specially for the party, and Charles is carrying in another tray of glasses. Mrs Upsilla goes in too, with two plates of tit-bits. Bacon wound round an apricot she makes, and sandwiches no bigger than a stamp. People come out and stand about on the landing. My mother and her friend are there for a moment, before she goes into the drawing-room again. He stays there, his shoulder against the wall by the window, the red curtains drawn over. 'The child's on to it,' was what he said the day before my father came back.

I don't want to go back to bed because the dream will be there even if I'm not asleep, Mrs Upsilla saying my father's gone for ever, that of course he had to. When I look for it, the leather suitcase he takes on his travels won't be there and I'll know it never will be again. I'll take out the Egyptian handkerchief and I'll remember my father spreading it on the café table, showing me the pattern. 'Our café,' he calls it.

My mother's friend looks up from the landing that's two flights down. He waves and I watch him coming up the stairs. There's a cigarette hanging from his mouth but he hasn't lit it and he doesn't take it out when he puts a finger to his lips. 'Enough to make them drunk,' Charles said when he saw the bottles opened on the kitchen table, and I wonder if my mother's friend is drunk because he takes another cigarette from his packet even though he hasn't lit the first one.

When he sways he has to reach out for the banister. He laughs, as if that's just for fun. I can see the sweat on his face, like raindrops on his forehead. His eyes are closed when he takes another step. Slowly he goes on coming up, another step and then another and another. There's a fleck of spit at the edge of his mouth, the two cigarettes have fallen on to the stair carpet. When I reach out I can touch him. My fingertips are on the dark cloth of his sleeve and I can feel his arm beneath, and everything is different then.

There is his tumbling down, there is the splintered banister. There is the thud, and then another and another. There is the stillness, and Mrs Upsilla looking up at me.

★

I watch them from my window, coming separately to the table they have chosen for breakfast in the garden of the hotel. They place their gifts by my place. They speak to one another, but I never know what they say in private. I turn from the window and powder over the coral lipstick I have just applied. On my seventeenth birthday nothing of my reflection is different in an oval looking-glass.

Downstairs, the salon I pass through is empty, the shutters half in place against the glare of sun that will be bothersome to the hotel guests later in the day.

'*Bonjour, mademoiselle,*' a waiter greets me in the garden.

Even in the early morning the air is mellow. Chestnuts have begun to fall; bright crimson leaves are shrivelling. The sky is cloudless.

'Well, old lady,' my father says. There is a single rose, pink bled with scarlet, which he has picked for me. On my birthday he always finds a rose somewhere.

'What shall we do today?' my mother asks when she

has poured my coffee and my father remembers the year of the Pilgrims' Way, when he took me on his back because I was tired, when we met the old man who told us about Saint Sisinnius. He remembers the balloon trip and the year of the casino. Birthdays are always an occasion, my mother's in July, my father's in May, mine in October.

We live in hotels. We've done so since we left the house in the square, all kinds of hotels, in the different countries of Europe, a temporary kind of life it seemed at first, acquiring permanence later.

'So what shall we do?' my mother asks again.

It is my choice because of the day and after I've opened the presents they've given me, after I've embraced them and thanked them, I say that what I'd like to do is to walk through the birch woods and have a picnic where the meadows begin.

'*Moi, je suis tous les sports,*' a man is telling his friend at the table next to ours. '*Il n'y en a pas un seul auquel je ne m' intéresse pas.*'

I can hear now, thirty-five years later, that man's rippling voice. I can see the face I glimpsed, bespectacled and pink, and hear his companion ordering *thé de Ceylan*.

'It will be lovely, that walk today,' my mother says, and we choose our picnic and after breakfast go to buy the different items and put our lunch together ourselves.

'Why do you always find a rose for me?'

I ask that on our walk, when my mother is quite far ahead of my father and myself. I have not chosen the moment; it is not because my mother isn't there; there's never anything like that.

'Oh, there isn't a reason for a rose, you know. It's just that sometimes a person wants to give one.'

'You make everything good for me.'

'Because it is your birthday.'

'I didn't mean only on my birthday.'

My mother has reached the meadows and calls back to us. When we catch up with her the picnic is already spread out, the wine uncorked.

'When your father and I first met,' she says once lunch has begun, 'he was buying a film for his camera and found himself short. That's how we met, in a little shop. He was embarrassed so I lent him a few coins from my purse.'

'Your mother has always had the money.'

'And it has never made a difference. An inheritance often does; but by chance, I think, this one never has.'

'No, it has never made a difference. But before we say another word we must drink a toast to today.'

My father pours the wine. 'You must not drink yourself, Villana. That isn't ever done.'

'Then may I have a toast to you? Is that ever done?'

'Well, do it and then it shall be.'

'Thank you for my birthday.'

In the sudden manner he often has my father says:

'Marco Polo was the first traveller to bring back to

Europe an account of the Chinese Empire. No one believed him. No one believed that the places he spoke of, or the people – not even Kublai Khan – existed. That is the history lesson for today, old lady. Or history and geography all in one. It doesn't matter how we think of it.'

'In German "to think" is *denken*,' my mother interposes. 'And in Italian?'

'*Pensare*. And *credere* of course.'

'This ham is delicious,' my father says.

They took me from England because that was best. I never went to school again. They taught me in their way, and between them they knew a lot: they taught me everything. My father's ambitions as an Egyptologist fell away. Once upon a time when he went on his travels – always determined to make discoveries that had not been made before – he scrimped and saved in order to be independent in his marriage, and in Egypt often slept on park benches. But after we left the house in the square my father had no profession; he became the amateur he once regarded as a status he despised. His books did not remain unwritten, but he did not ever want to publish them.

'Oh, how good this is!' he says, his soft voice hardly heard when my birthday picnic is over, the wine all drunk. We lie, all three of us, in the warm autumn sun, and then I pack the remains of the picnic into the haversack and think that my father is right, that this is good, even that it is happiness.

'I worry sometimes he does not get enough exercise,' my mother remarks on our journey back, going by a different way, my father's turn now to be a little ahead. Often, it seems to me, it is deliberately arranged that I should always be in the company of one or other of them.

'Doesn't he get enough?'

'Well, it could be more.'

'Papa's not ill?'

'No, not at all. Not at all. But in the nature of things . . .'

She does not finish what she might have said, but I know what follows. In the nature of things neither she nor my father will always be there. I sense her guessing that I have finished her sentence for her, for that is how we live, our conversations incomplete, or never begun at all. They have between them created an artefact within which our existence lies, an artefact as scrupulously completed as a masterpiece on a mosaicist's table. My father accepts what he has come to know – which I believe is everything – of my mother's unfaithfulness. There is no regret on my mother's part that I can tell, nor is there bitterness on his; I never heard a quarrel. They sacrifice their lives for me: the change of surroundings, constantly repeated, the anonymous furniture of hotels, nothing as it has been – for my sake, no detail is overlooked. In thanking them I might say my gratitude colours every day, but they do not want me to say that, not even to mention gratitude in such a manner because it would be too much.

'Quel après-midi splendide!'
'Ah, oui! on peut le dire.'
'J'adore ce moment de la journée.'

Often my mother and I break into one of the languages she has taught me; as if, for her, a monotony she does not permit is broken. Does she – do they – regret the loss of the house in London, as I do? Do they imagine the changes there might be, the blue hall door a different colour, business plates beside it, a voice on the intercom when one of the bells is rung? What is the drawing-room now? Is there a consulate in the ground-floor rooms, stately men going back and forth, secretaries with papers to be signed? All that I know with certainty – and they must too – is that the violets of my bedroom wallpaper have been painted away to nothing, that gone from the hall are the shipyard scenes in black and white, the Cries of London too. They may even wonder, as I do, if the chill of the past is in that house, if the ghosts of my childhood companions haunt its rooms, for since leaving England I have never been able to bring them to life again.

'C'est vraiment très beau là-bas,' my mother says when we catch up with my father, who has already begun to gather chestnuts. We watch a bird which he says is something rare, none of us knowing what it is. There is a boy at the hotel to whom we'll give the chestnuts, each of us knowing as we do so that this will become another birthday memory, spoken of, looked back to.

'Ernest Shackleton was a most remarkable man,' my

father comments in his abrupt way. 'Maybe the finest of all those men who were remarkable for making the freezing winds a way of life, and ice a landscape, whose grail was the desolation at the end of the world's most terrible journeys. Can you imagine them, those men before him and all who followed later? Secrets kept from one another, ailments hidden, their prayers, their disappointments? Such adversity, yet such spirit! We are strangely made, we human beings, don't you think?'

It doesn't matter that he hasn't taken me to see the Pyramids, not in the least does it matter, but even so I do not ever say I understand why he hasn't. For that, of course, is best not said. I, too, prevaricate.

'We've never brought you to Heiligenberg,' he muses as we walk on.

The last of the autumn wild flowers would still be in bloom at Heiligenberg, and the hellebores out all winter. The hotel they know – the Zeldenhof – would be grander since their day, my mother says.

We'll spend the winter in Heiligenberg, they decide, and I wonder if at Heiligenberg a letter might come from Mrs Upsilla. Now and again, not often, one arrives at some hotel or is discovered at a *Poste Restante*. Once I saw what I knew I should not have: the cramped handwriting I remembered, the purple ink Mrs Upsilla always favoured. Such letters that come are never opened in my presence; once when I looked in my mother's belongings none had been kept.

'We stayed at the Zeldenhof when we were married

a month,' my father says. 'I photographed your mother at the refuge.'

I ask about that, and I ask where the little shop was where they met, when my father was buying a film for his camera.

'Italy,' my mother says. 'The front at Bordighera.'

There is a photograph.

★

The ticket collector's beard is flecked with grey, his uniform in need of attention. I know him well, for often I travel on his train.

'*Grazie, signora.*' He hands my ticket back, reminding me to change in Milan and Genoa. In the early after-noon the string of little seaside towns will begin, the train unhurried then, slowing, halting, juddering on, gathering speed again. That part of the journey I like best.

I wear blue because it suits me best, often with green, although they say the two are difficult to combine. My hair's well tended, the style old-fashioned. 'You're an old-fashioned lady,' my father used to say, not chiding me for that, his tone as light as ever. She liked my old-fashionedness, my mother said when I was very young. I'm in my fifty-third year now, a woman who has settled down at last in the forgotten Italian seaside resort where they met. In nineteen forty-nine that was, I calculate.

They died, he first – in his eighties – she less than a year later; and I, who should have known them better than anyone, did not know them at all, even though my mother did not release my hand all during her last night. The second funeral was conducted with the same simple formality as the first, the coffin placed beside the other in the small graveyard they had chosen, the place remembered from the summers we often spent in the Valle Verzasca. I walked away from both of them through cold winter air, snow on the ground but no longer falling.

A month or so later, calling in at the *Poste Restante* at Bad Mergentheim, as we had always done in their lifetime, I found a letter from Mrs Upsilla. Addressed as usual to my mother, it had been lying there for almost a year.

> . . . *I only write because it is so long now since I have heard from you. I am concerned but perhaps it is all right and you have been so kind to an old woman. The summer has not been good in Brighton but I struggle on, the season very poor. Several other landladies have given up and I read the writing on the wall and think how different life was once, those days in London! Well, I must not say it but there you are. I only write because I have not heard.*

I knew at once that my mother had paid Mrs Upsilla all these years. Charles too, I imagined. The rich's desperate bid for silence: I think of it as that; but no, I do not blame my mother. I replied to Mrs Upsilla, simply saying that my mother had died and asking her to pass this information on to Charles if she happened to be in touch with him. No acknowledgement ever found its way to me from either of them, but it was hearing from Mrs Upsilla that first made me want to honour my father and mother. For Mrs Upsilla would die too, and Charles would, and I myself in time: who then, in all the world, would be aware of the story that might be told?

In the hotel where I live, in Bordighera's Regina Palace, my friends are the dining-room waiters, and the porters in the hall, and the bedroom maids; I do not turn away such friendship and I have myself for company too. Yet when my face is there in the glass of my compact, or reflected in shop windows when the sun is right, or glimpsed in public mirrors, I often think I do not know that woman. I wonder when I gaze for a moment longer if what I see is the illusion imposed by my imagination upon the shadow a child became, if somehow I do not entirely exist. I know that this is not so, yet still it seems to be. Confusion has coloured my life since my mother's death; and the waking hours of my solitude are nagged by the compulsion to make known the goodness of two people. Obsessively there, beyond my understanding, that has become the insistent orderer of how things should be. Not ever finding the courage to make it known in the corridors and lounges of the Regina

Palace, for years I travelled from my shabby old town by the sea to distant cities where I might be anonymous. Again and again I searched among strangers for a listener who would afterwards pass on as a wonder the beneficence of those two people, a marvel to be repeated at family gatherings, at dinner tables, in bars and shops, interrupting games of cards and chess, spreading to other cities, to villages and towns, to other countries.

Each time I found my listener, each time across a teashop table or in a park, there was politeness; and moments later there was revulsion. Some traveller killing tedious time in a railway waiting-room would look away and mumble nothing; or on a tram, or in a train, would angrily push past a nuisance. And the whisper of my apology would not be heard.

In my foolishness I did not know what I since have learnt: that the truth, even when it glorifies the human spirit, is hard to peddle if there is something terrible to tell as well. Dark nourishes light's triumphant blaze, but who should want to know? I accept, at last, that I am not to be allowed the mercy of telling what is mine to tell. The wheels of my suitcase rattle on the surface of the railway platform at Bordighera and outside the station the evening is bright with sunshine. The taxi-driver knows my destination without having to ask. I might say, in making conversation, that there will not be another journey but enquire instead about the family he often tells me about.

'*Buona sera, signora. Come sta?*' The afternoon porter welcomes me in the empty hall of the Regina Palace, appearing out of nowhere.

'*Sto bene, Giovanni. Bene.*'

Small and pallid, an elaborate uniform dwarfing him, Giovanni keeps the Regina Palace going, as much as Signor Valazza, its manager, does; or the stoutly imperious Signora Casarotti, who knew it from her Reception counter in its glory days. Fashion has long ago lifted its magic from what fashion once made gracious, leaving behind flaking paint and dusty palms. Masonry crumbles, a forgotten lift is out of order. But Camera Ventinove, the room I have always returned to from the failure of my journeys, has a view of the sea as far as the horizon.

'We miss you always, *signora*,' Giovanni tells me, practising his English, as he likes to in our conversations. 'Was fine, your travel, *signora?*'

'Was fine, Giovanni, was fine.'

The door of Camera Ventinove is unlocked as that lie is told. Giovanni stands aside, I go in first. There is a little more to the ceremony of my return, not much: the opening of the shutters, the view again remarked upon, the giving and receiving of the tip. Then Giovanni goes.

I hang some of the clothes I have travelled with in the wardrobe and write the list to accompany those that must be laundered. Unhurriedly, I have a bath and, downstairs for a while, finish the easy book I bought for my journey. I leave it with the newspapers in case it interests someone else.

I walk by the sea, my thoughts a repetition, imagining on this promenade the two people who have been rejected, who did not know one another well when they walked here too. The bathing huts of the photograph have gone.

'*Buona sera, signora.*'

It is not an unusual courtesy for people to address one another on this promenade, even for a man who is not familiar to her to address a woman. But still this unexpected voice surprises me, and perhaps I seem a little startled.

'I'm sorry, I did not mean to . . .' The man's apology trails away.

'It's quite all right.'

'We are both English, I think.' His voice is soft, pleasant to hear, his eyes quite startling blue. He is tall, in a pale linen suit, thin and fair-haired, his forehead freckled, the blue of his eyes repeated in the tie that's knotted into a blue-striped shirt. Some kindly doctor? Schoolmaster? Horticulturalist? Something about him suggests he's on his own. Widowed? I wondered. Unmarried? It is impossible to guess. His name is d'Arblay, he reveals, and when I begin to walk on, it seems only slightly strange that he changes direction and walks with me.

'Yes, I am English,' I hear myself saying, more warmly than if I had not hesitated at first.

'I thought you might be. Well, I knew. But even so it was a presumption.' The slightest of gestures accompanies this variation of his apology. He smiles a little. 'My thoughts had wandered. I was thinking as I strolled of a novel I first read when I was eighteen. *The Good Soldier*.'

'I have read *The Good Soldier* too.'

'The saddest story. I read it again not long ago. You've read it more than once?'

'Yes, I have.'

'There's always something that wasn't there before when you read a good novel for the second time.'

'Yes, there is.'

'I have been re-reading now the short stories of Somerset Maugham. Superior to his novels, I believe. In particular I like "The Kite".'

'They made a film of it.'

'Yes.'

'I never saw it.'

'Nor I.'

There is no one else on the promenade. Neither a person nor a dog. Not even a seagull. We walk together, not speaking for a moment, until I break that silence, not to say much, but only that I love the sea at Bordighera.

'And I.'

Our footsteps echo, or somehow do I imagine that? I don't know, am only aware that again the silence is there, and that again I break it.

'A long time ago I lived in a house in a square in London . . .'

He nods, but does not speak.

'My father was an Egyptologist.'

★

Taped music reaches me in the bar, where once there was the chatter of cocktail drinkers and the playing of a palm-court quartet. I order Kir, and when the barman has poured it he leaves me on my own, as every night he does, since he has other things to do. I guessed this would be so and for company I've brought with me the temperate features of the Englishman on the promenade. 'So much is chance,' he said, and with no great difficulty I hear his distinctive voice again. 'So much,' he says.

I take that with me when I cross the hall to the struggling splendours of the Regina Palace's dining-room. I take with me Mr d'Arblay's composure, his delicate hands seeming to gesture without moving, the smile that is so slight it's hardly there. Royalty has celebrated in this vast dining-room, so Signor Valazza claims. But tonight's reflection in its gilded mirrors is a handful of travellers, shadowy beneath the flickering chandeliers. There is a man with a yellow pipe on the table beside him, and a couple who might be on their honeymoon, and two ageing German *fräuleins* who might be schoolmistresses just retired. Little stoves keep warm *filetto di maialino* and *tortelli di pecorino*. But all reality is less than Mr d'Arblay.

'*Si, signora.*' Carlo jots down my order: the consommé, the turbot. '*E Gavi dei Gavi. Subito, signora.*'

My mother gathered her dress from the floor, her necklace too, where she had thrown them down. The drawing-room was heavy with her scent and her friend put a record on the gramophone. The voice still sang when they had gone. And Charles came in then, and knew, and took me out to the square to show me the flowerbeds he'd been tending.

'*Prego, signora. Il vino.*'

The Gavi is poured, but I do not need to taste it, and simply nod.

'*Grazie, signora.*'

Mr d'Arblay has walked through our square; more than once he remembers being there. It is not difficult for him to imagine the house as it was; he does not say so, but I know. He can imagine; he is the kind that can.

'*Buon appetito, signora.*'

A child's light fingertips on a sleeve, resting there for no longer than an instant. So swift her movement then, so slight it might not have occurred at all: that, too, Mr d'Arblay can imagine and he does. The unlit cigarettes are crushed beneath a shoe. There is the crash of noise, the splintered banister. There are the eyes, looking up from far below. There is the rictus grin.

The man on his own presses tobacco into his yellow pipe but does not light it. Ice-cream is brought to the German schoolmistresses. The honeymoon couple touch glasses. Three late arrivals hesitate by the door.

'*Il rombo arrosto, signora.*'

'*Grazie, Carlo.*'

'*Prego, signora.*'

Three lives were changed for ever in that instant. Whatever lies my father told were good enough for people at a party, the silence of two servants bought. My mother wept and hid her tears. But some time during that sleepless night was she – my father too – touched by the instinct to abandon the child who had been born to them? Was it more natural that they should, and do no more than call what had happened evil?

'It is natural too,' Mr d'Arblay replied while we walked, 'to find the truth in the agony of distress. The innocent cannot be evil: this was what, during that sleepless night, they came to know.'

It was enough, Mr d'Arblay diffidently insisted, that what there is to tell, in honouring the dead, has now been told between two other people and shall be told again between them, and each time something gained. The selfless are undemanding in their graves.

I do not taste the food I'm eating, nor savour the wine I drink. I reject the *dolce* and the cheese. They bring me coffee.

'Theirs was the guilt,' Mr d'Arblay says again, 'his that he did not know her well enough, hers that she made the most of his not knowing. Theirs was the shame, yet their spirit is gentle in our conversation: guilt is not always terrible, nor shame unworthy.'

Petits fours have been brought too, although I never take one from the plate. One night she may, is what they think in the kitchen, and even say to one another that one night when she sits down at this same table, as old as she will ever become, she will be lonely in her solitude. How can they know that in the dining-room where royalty has dined she is not alone among the tattered drapes and chandeliers abandoned to their grime? They cannot know, they cannot guess, that in the old hotel, and when she walks by the sea, there is Mr d'Arblay, as in another solitude there were her childhood friends.

Sacred Statues

They would manage, Nuala had always said when there had been difficulties before. Each time it was she who saw the family through: her faith in Corry, her calmness in adversity, her stubborn optimism were the strengths she brought to the marriage.

'Would you try Mrs Falloway?' she suggested when, more seriously than ever in the past, their indigence threatened to defeat them. It was a last resort, the best that desperation could do. 'Wouldn't you, Corry?'

Corry said nothing and Nuala watched him feeling ashamed, as he had begun to these last few weeks. It wouldn't be asking much of Mrs Falloway, she said. Tiding them over for a year while he learnt the way of it in the stoneyard wouldn't be much; and after that he'd be back on wages. The chance in the stoneyard was made for him; didn't O'Flynn say it himself?

'I couldn't go near Mrs Falloway. I couldn't at all.'

'Only to put it to her, Corry. Only to say out what's the truth.'

'It came to nothing, what she was doing that time. Why'd she be interested in us now?'

'All she saw in you'll be lost if we don't get assistance, Corry. Why wouldn't she still take an interest?'

'It's all in the past, that.'

'I know. I know.'

'I'd be embarrassed going over there.'

'Don't I know that too, Corry?'

'There's work going on the roads.'

'You're not a roadworker, Corry.'

'There's things we have to do.'

Deliberately Nuala let a silence gather; and Corry broke it, as she knew he would.

'I'd be a day going over there,' he said, and might have added that there'd be the bus fare and something to pay for the loan of a bicycle in Carrick, but he didn't.

'A day won't hurt, Corry.'

They were a couple of the same age – thirty-one – who'd known one another since childhood, Corry tall and bony, Nuala plumper and smaller, with a round, uncomplicated face, her fair hair cut shorter than it had been when she'd first become a wife. The youngest of their children, a girl, took after her in appearance; the boys were both as lean and gangling as their father.

'You always did your best, Corry.' The statement hung there, concluding their conversation, necessary because it was true, its repetition softening the crisis in their lives.

*

Corry's workshop was a shed, all his saints in a row on a shelf he had put up. Beneath them were his

Madonnas, his John the Baptist, and a single Cruci-
fixion. His Stations were there too, propped against the
rough concrete wall. Limewood and ash the woods
were, apple and holly and box, oak that had come from
a creamery paddle.

When the children left the house in the mornings to
be picked up at Quirke's crossroads and driven on to
school, when Corry was out looking for work on a
farm, Nuala often took pride in her husband's gift; and
in the quiet of his workshop she wondered how it
would have been between them if he did not possess
it, how she would feel about him if he'd been the
master in a school or a counter-hand in one of the
shops in Carrick, or permanently on a farm.

Corry's saints had become her friends, Nuala sometimes thought, brought to life for her, a source of sympathy, and consolation when that was necessary. *And
Jesus Fell the Second Time* were the words beneath the
Station that was her favourite. Neither saints nor
Stations belonged in a concrete shed, any more than the
figures of the Virgin did, or any of the other carvings.
They belonged in the places they'd been created for, the
inspiration of their making becoming there the inspiration of prayer. Nuala was certain that this was meant
to be, that in receiving his gift Corry had been entrusted
with seeing that this came about. 'You were meant for
other times, Corry,' a priest had remarked to him once,
but not unkindly or dismissively, as if recognizing that
even if the present times were different from those he

spoke of, Corry would persevere. A waste of himself it would be otherwise, a waste of the person he was.

Nuala closed the shed door behind her. She fed her hens and then walked through the vegetable patch she cultivated herself. Mrs Falloway would understand; she had before, she would again. The living that Corry's gift failed to make for him would come naturally when he had mastered the craft of cutting letters on headstones in O'Flynn's yard. The headstones were a different kind of thing from his sacred statues but they'd be enough to bring his skill to people's notice, to the notice of bishops and priests as well as anyone else's. Sooner or later everyone did business in a stoneyard; when he'd come to the house to make the offer O'Flynn had said that too.

In the field beyond Nuala's vegetable garden the tethered goat jerked up its head and stared at her. She loosened the chain on the tether post and watched while the goat pawed at the new grass before eating it. The fresh, cool air was sharp on her face and for a moment, in spite of the trouble, she was happy. At least this place was theirs: the field, the garden, the small, remote house that she and Corry had come to when Mrs Falloway lent them the asking price, so certain was she that Corry would one day be a credit to her. While still savouring this moment of elation, Nuala felt it slipping away. Naturally, it was possible that Corry would not succeed in the mission she had sent him on: optimist or not, she was still close to the reality of things. In the night she had struggled with that, wondering how she should prepare him, and herself, for the ill fortune of his coming back empty-handed. It was then that she had remembered the Rynnes. They'd come into her thoughts as she imagined an inspiration came to Corry; not that he ever talked like that, but still she felt she knew. She had lain awake going over what had occurred to her, rejecting it because it upset her, because it shocked her even to have thought of it. She prayed that Mrs Falloway would be generous, as she had been before.

*

When he reached the crossroads Corry waited at the petrol pumps for the bus to Carrick. It was late but it didn't matter, since Mrs Falloway didn't know he was coming. On the way down from the house he'd considered trying to telephone, to put it to her if she was still there what Nuala had put to him, to save himself the expense of the journey. But when first she'd brought the subject up, Nuala had said that this wasn't something that could be talked about on the phone even if he managed to find out Mrs Falloway's number, which he hadn't known in the past.

In Carrick, at Hosey's bicycle shop, he waited while the tyres of an old Raleigh were pumped up for him. New batteries were put in the lamp in case he returned after dark, although he kept assuring young Hosey that it wouldn't be possible to be away for so long: the bus back was at three.

It was seven miles to Mountroche House, mostly on a flat bog road bounded by neither ditches nor fencing. Corry remembered it from the time he and Nuala had lived in Carrick, when he'd worked in the Riordans' joinery business and they'd had lodgings in an upstairs room at her mother's. It was then that he began to carve his statues, his instinctive artistry impressing the Riordan brothers, and Mrs Falloway when the time came. It surprised Corry himself, for he hadn't known it was there.

Those times, the first few years of marriage, cheered him as he rode swiftly on. It could be that Nuala was right, that Mrs Falloway would be pleased to see him, that she'd understand why they hadn't been able to pay anything back. Nuala had a way of making good things happen, Corry considered; she guessed what they might be and then you tried for them.

The road was straight, with hardly a curve until the turf bogs eventually gave way to hills. Hedges and trees began, fields of grass or crops. Mountroche House was at the end of an unkempt avenue that continued for another three-quarters of a mile.

★

The Rynnes lived in a grey, pebble-dashed bungalow at the crossroads, close to the petrol pumps they operated, across the main road from Quirke's SuperValu. They were well-to-do: besides the petrol business, there was Rynne's insurance agency, which he conducted from the bungalow. His wife attended to the custom at the pumps.

When Nuala rang the doorbell the Rynnes answered it together. They had a way of doing that when both of them were in; and they had a way of conducting their visitors no further than the hall until the purpose of the interruption was established. An insurance matter was usually enough to permit further access.

'I was passing by,' Nuala said, 'on my way to the SuperValu.'

The Rynnes nodded. Their similar elongated features suggested that they might be brother and sister rather than man and wife. They both wore glasses, Rynne's dark-rimmed and serious, his wife's light and pale. They were a childless couple.

'Is it insurance, Nuala?' Rynne enquired.

She shook her head. She'd just looked in, she said, to see how they were getting on. 'We often mention you,' she said, taking a liberty with the facts.

'Arrah, we're not bad at all,' Rynne said. 'Game ball, would you say, Etty?'

'Oh, I would, I would.'

The telephone rang and Rynne went to answer it. Nuala could hear him saying he was up to his eyes this morning. 'Would tomorrow do?' he suggested. 'Would I come up in the evening?'

'I'm sorry, Etty. You're busy.'

'It's only I'm typing his proposals. God, it takes your time, and the pumps going too! Twenty-six blooming pages every one of them!'

In spite of its plaintive note, it was cheerful talk, relegating to its place beneath the surface what had been disguised when Rynne said they were game ball: neither Etty Rynne's failure to become pregnant nor the emotional toll it had taken of both husband and wife was ever mentioned by them, but the fact and its consequences were well known in the neighbourhood. It was even said that dishearteningly fruitless enquiries had been made regarding the possibility of adoption.

'Goodbye so, Etty.' Nuala smiled and nodded before she left, the sympathy of a mother in her eyes. She would have liked to commiserate, but spoken words would have been tactless.

'You're all well above, Nuala?'

'We are.'

'Tell Corry I was asking for him.'

'I will of course.'

Nuala wheeled her bicycle across the road and propped it against the side wall of Quirke's SuperValu. While she was shopping – searching for the cheap lines with a sell-by date due, bundling the few items she could afford into a wire basket – she thought about the Rynnes. She saw them almost as visibly as she had ten minutes ago seen the faraway, sorrowful look in Etty's pale-brown eyes; she heard the unvoiced disappointment that, in both husband and wife, dwindled into weariness. They had given up already, not knowing that they needn't yet: all that, again, passed through Nuala's reflections.

She went on thinking about the Rynnes as she rode away from the crossroads, up the long hill to her house. They were decent people, tied into themselves only because of their childlessness, because of what the longing had done to them. She remembered them as they'd been when first they'd married, the winter card parties they invited people to, Etty like a fashion-plate for each occasion, the stories Rynne brought back from his business travels.

'Would it be wrong?' Nuala whispered to herself, since there was no one there to hear. 'Would it be against God?'

Unhooking her shopping bags from the handlebars when she reached the house, she asked herself the same questions again, her voice loud now in the stillness. If Corry did well with Mrs Falloway there wouldn't be a need to wonder if it would be wrong. There wouldn't even be a need – when years had gone by and they looked back to the bad time there'd been – to mention to Corry what had come into her mind. If Mrs Falloway came up trumps you'd make yourself forget it, which was something that could be done if you tried.

★

It was a white house for the most part, though grey and green in places where the colourwash was affected. Roches had lived at Mountroche for generations, until the family came to an end in the 1950s; Mrs Falloway had bought it cheaply after it had been empty for seventeen years.

Corry heard the bell jangling in the depths, but no one answered the summons. On the bus and as he rode across the bog he had worried in case Mrs Falloway had gone, in case years ago she had returned to England; when he jerked the bell-pull for the third time he worried again. Then there was a sound somewhere above where he stood. A window opened and Mrs Falloway's voice called down.

'Mrs Falloway?' He stepped backwards on to the gravel in order to look up. 'Mrs Falloway?'

'Yes, it's me. Hullo.'

'Hullo, Mrs Falloway.'

He wouldn't have recognized her and wondered if she recognized him after so long. He said who he was.

'Oh, of course,' Mrs Falloway said. 'Wait a minute for me.'

When she opened her hall door she was welcoming. She smiled and held a hand out. 'Come in, come in.'

They passed through a shabby hall and sat in a drawing-room that smelt of must. The cold ashes of a fire were partly covered with dead hydrangeas, deposited there from a vase. The room seemed choked

with what littered its surfaces: newspapers and magazines, drawings, books face downward as if to mark a
place, empty punnets, bric-à-brac in various stages of
repair, a summer hat, a pile of clothes beside a work-
basket.

'You've come on a bicycle, Corry?' Mrs Falloway
said.

'Only from Carrick. I got the bus to Carrick.'

'My dear, you must be exhausted. Let me give you
tea at the very least.'

Mrs Falloway was gone for nearly twenty minutes,
causing Corry some agitation when he thought of the
three o'clock bus. He and Nuala had sat waiting in this
room when they'd come to the house the first time,
after Corry got the letter. They'd sat together on the
sofa that was a receptacle for oddments now; the room
had been tidier then, Mrs Falloway had been brisker.
She'd talked all the time, full of her plans, a table laid
in the big bow window to which she brought corned
beef and salad, and toast that was moist with the butter
she'd spread, and Kia-Ora orange, and tea and fruitcake.

'Not much, I'm afraid,' she said now, returning with
a plate of biscuits, and cups and saucers and a teapot. The biscuits were decorated with a pink mush of
marshmallow and raspberry jam.

Corry was glad of the tea, which was strong and hot.
The biscuit he took had gone soft, but even so he liked
it. Once in a while Nuala bought the same kind for the
children.

'What a lovely surprise!' Mrs Falloway said.

'I wondered were you still here.'

'I'm here for ever now, I think.'

A dismal look had crept into her face, as if she knew why he had come. If she'd thought about it, she would have guessed long ago about the plight they were in. He wasn't here to say it was her fault; he hoped she didn't think that, because of course it wasn't. All the blame was his.

'I'm sorry we didn't manage to pay anything back,' he said.

'You weren't expected to, Corry.'

She was a tall woman, seeming fragile now. When she'd been younger her appearance had been almost intimidating: determination had influenced the set of her features and seemed to be there again in her wide mouth and saucer eyes, in her large hands as they gestured for attention. Swiftly her smile had become stern or insistent; now it was vaguely beseeching; her piled-up hair, which Corry remembered as black with a few strands of grey, had no black left in it. There was a tattered look about her that went with the room they were in.

'You have children now, Corry?'

'We have three. Two boys and a girl.'

'You're finding work?'

He shook his head. 'It never got going,' he said. 'All that.'

'I'm sorry, Corry.'

Soon after Mrs Falloway bought Mountroche House and came to live there she had attended the funeral of the elderly widow who'd been the occupant of the Mountroche gate-lodge. Being, as she put it, a black Protestant from England, who had never, until then, entered an Irish Catholic church, she had not before been exposed to such a profusion of plaster statues as at that funeral Mass. *I hope you do not consider it interference from an outsider*, she wrote in her first letter to Bishop Walshe, *but it is impossible not to be aware of the opportunity there is for young craftsmen and artists.* With time on her hands, she roved Bishop Walshe's diocese in her Morris Minor, taking photographs of grottoes that featured solitary Virgin Marys or *pietàs*, or towering crucifixions. How refreshing it would be, she enthused to Bishop Walshe when eventually she visited him, to see the art of the great high crosses of Ireland brought into the modern Church, to see nativities and annunciations in stained glass, to have old lecterns and altar furniture replaced with contemporary forms. She left behind in the Bishop's hall a selection of postcards she had obtained from Italy, reproductions of the bas-reliefs of Mino da Fiesole and details from the pulpit in Siena cathedral. When she had compiled a list of craftsmen she wrote to all of them, and visited those who lived within a reasonable distance of Mountroche House. To numerous priests and bishops she explained that what was necessary was to bring wealth and talent together; but for the most part she met with opposition and indifference. Several bishops wrote back crossly, requesting her not to approach them again.

Breaking in half another biscuit, Corry remembered the letter he had received himself. 'Will you look at this!' he had exclaimed the morning it arrived. Since he had begun to carve figures in his spare time at the joinery he had been aware of a vocation, of wishing to make a living in this particular way, and Mrs Falloway's letter reflected entirely what he felt: that the church art with which he was familiar was of poor quality. 'Who on earth is she?' he wondered in bewilderment when he'd read the letter through several times. Less than a week later Mrs Falloway came to introduce herself.

'I've always been awfully sorry,' she repeated now. 'Sorrier than I can say.'

'Ah, well.'

When it was all over, all her efforts made, her project abandoned, Mrs Falloway had written in defeat to a friend of her distant schooldays. *Well, yes, I am giving up the struggle. There is a long story to tell, which must wait until next you come for a few summer weeks. Enough to say, that everything has changed in holy Ireland.* Mrs Falloway spoke of that to Corry now, of her feelings at the time, which she had not expressed to him before. The Church had had enough on its hands, was how she put it; the appearance of things seemed trivial compared with the falling away of congregations and the tide of secular attack. Without knowing it, she had chosen a bad time.

'It was guilt when I gave you that poor little house, Corry. I'd misled you with my certainties that weren't certainties at all. A galumphing English woman!'

'Ah no, no.'

'Ah yes, I'm afraid. I should have restrained you, not urged you to give up your employment in the joinery.'

'I wanted to.'

'You're hard up now?'

'We are a bit, to tell the truth.'

'Is that why you've come over?'

'Well, it is.'

She shook her head. There was another pause and then she said: 'I'm hard up myself, as things are.'

'I'm sorry about that.'

'Are you in a bad way, Corry?'

'O'Flynn'll give me a place in the stoneyard at Guileen. He's keen because I'd learn the stone quickly, the knowledge I have with the wood. It's not like he'd be taking on a full apprentice. It's not like the delay there'd be until some young fellow'd get the hang of it.'

'You'd be lettering gravestones?'

'I would. He'd put me on wages after a twelve-month. The only thing is, I'd be the twelve-month without a penny. I do a few days on a farm here and there if there's anything going, but I'd have to give that up.'

'The stoneyard seems the answer then.'

'I'd be in touch with anyone who'd maybe be interested in the statues. I'd have them by me in the yard. A priest or a bishop still looking for something would maybe hear tell I could do a Stations. O'Flynn said that to Nuala.'

They went on talking. Mrs Falloway poured out more tea. She pressed Corry to have another biscuit.

'I'd have the wages steady behind me,' Corry said, 'once we managed the year. I'd ride over to Guileen every morning on the bike we have, no problem at all.'

'I haven't money, Corry.'

There was a quietness in the room then, neither of them saying anything, but Corry didn't go at once. After a few moments they talked about the time in the past. Mrs Falloway offered to cook something, but Corry said no. He stood up as he did so, explaining about the three o'clock bus.

At the hall door Mrs Falloway again said she was sorry, and Corry shook his head.

'Nuala's tried for work herself only there's nothing doing. There's another baby coming,' Corry said, feeling he should pass that on also.

*

When Nuala heard, she said it had been a forlorn hope anyway, and when Corry described the state of Mountroche House she felt sorry for Mrs Falloway, whose belief in Corry had always seemed to Nuala to be a confirmation of the sacred nature of his gift, as if Mrs Falloway had been sent into their lives to offer that encouragement. Even though her project had failed, it was hardly by chance that she had come to live only fourteen miles from Carrick at a time when Corry was employed in the Riordans' joinery; and hardly by chance that she'd become determined in her intentions when she saw the first of his saints. He'd made the little figure of St Brigid for Father Ryan to set in the niche in St Brigid's parish hall even though Father Ryan couldn't pay him anything for it. Whenever Nuala was in Carrick she called in at the parish hall to look again at it, remembering her amazement – similar to Mrs Falloway's – when she'd first seen it. 'He has a right way with a chisel,' O'Flynn said when he'd made his offer of employment in the stoneyard. 'I don't know did I ever see better.' For Nuala it was all of a piece – the first of the saints, and Mrs Falloway coming to live near by, and O'Flynn's offer when they'd nearly given up hope. She could feel it in her bones that that was how it was.

'Rest yourself,' she urged Corry in the kitchen, 'while I'll get the tea.'

'They all right?'

They were out playing in the back field, she said; they'd been no trouble since they'd come in. She spread out rashers of streaky bacon on the pan that was warming on the stove. She'd gone down to the Super-

Valu, she said, and Corry told her how he'd nearly missed the bus back.

'He was drawing away. I had to stop him.'

'I shouldn't have sent you over on that awful old trek, Corry.'

'Ah no, no. To tell you the truth, it was good to see her. Except she was a bit shook.'

He talked about the journey on the bus, the people on it when he was coming back. Nuala didn't mention the Rynnes.

*

'Glory be to God!' Etty Rynne exclaimed. She felt shaky so she sat down, on a chair by the hallstand. 'I don't think I understood you,' she said, although she knew she had.

She listened, not wanting to, when Nuala went into it. 'It'd be April,' Nuala said and repeated the sum of money she had mentioned already. Late April, she thought, maybe just into May. She'd never been early, she said.

'Himself would say it was against the law, Nuala. I'd wonder was it, myself.'

The daylight in the hall had blurs of blue and pink in it from the coloured panes on either side of the front door. It was a dim, soft light because of that, and while she tried to gather her thoughts together Etty Rynne found herself thinking that its cloudiness was suitable for the conversation that was being conducted – neither of them able to see the other's face clearly, her own incomprehension.

'It would be confidential between us,' Nuala said, 'that there was money.'

Not meaning to, and in a whisper, Etty Rynne repeated that. A secret was what was meant: a secret kept for ever among the four of them, a secret that was begun already because Nuala had waited for the car to drive off, maybe watching from the SuperValu's windows. She'd have seen him walking out of the bungalow; when the car had gone she'd have crossed the road.

'Listen to me, Etty.'

Corry's statues came into what Nuala said, the wooden figures he made, the Blessed Virgin and the saints, St Brigid in the St Brigid's Hall in Carrick. And Nuala trying for work in the SuperValu and anywhere she could think of came into it. With the baby due she'd be tied down, but she'd have managed somehow if there was work, only there wasn't. How Corry had drawn a blank with a woman whose name was unfamiliar came into it. And O'Flynn who had the stoneyard at Guileen did.

'O'Flynn has his insurances with us.' For a moment in her mind's eye Etty Rynne saw the bulky grey-haired stonemason, who always dropped the premiums in himself in case they went astray, who afterwards drew his Peugeot pick-up in at the pumps for a fill-up. It was a relief when all that flickered in Etty Rynne's memory, after the shock that had left her weak in the legs and wanting to gasp and not being able to.

'It's a long time since you put the room ready, Etty.'

'Did I show it to you?'

'You did one time.'

She used to show it to people, the small room at the back of the bungalow that she'd painted a bright buttercup shade, the door and windowsills in white gloss.

'It's still the same,' she said.

'That's what I was thinking.'

She'd made the curtains herself, blue that matched the carpet, dolls playing ring-a-roses on them. They'd never bought furniture for the little room. Tempting Providence it would be, he said.

'There'd be no deception,' Nuala said. 'No lie, nothing like that. Only the money side kept out of it.'

Etty nodded. Like a dream, it was disordered and peculiar: the ring at the door and Nuala smiling there, and standing in the hall with Nuala and having to sit down, her face going red and then the blood draining out of it when Nuala asked if she had savings in the bank or in a credit society, and mentioning the sum that would be enough.

'I couldn't take your baby off of you, Nuala.'

'I wouldn't be deprived. I'd have another one, maybe two or three. A bit of time gone by and people would understand.'

'Oh God, I doubt they would.'

'It isn't against the law, Etty. No way.'

'I couldn't. I never could.' Pregnancy made you fanciful sometimes and she wondered if it was that that had got at Nuala. She didn't say it in case it made things worse. Slowly she shook her head. 'God, I couldn't,' she said again.

'Nowadays if a man and woman can't have a baby there's things can be done.'

'I know, I know.'

'Nowadays –'

'I couldn't do what you're saying, Nuala.'

'Is it the money?'

'It's everything, Nuala. It's what people'd say. He'd blow his head off if he knew what you're after suggesting. It would bring down the business, he'd say. Nobody'd come near us.'

'People –'

'They'd never come round to it, Nuala.'

A silence came, and the silence was worse than the talk. Then Nuala said:

'Would we sit down to a cup of coffee?'

'God, I'm sorry. Of course we will.'

She could feel sweat on the sides of her body and on her neck and her forehead. The palms of her hands were cold. She stood up and it was better than before.

'Come into the kitchen.'

'I didn't mean to upset you, Etty.'

Filling the kettle, spooning Nescafé into two cups,

pouring in milk, Etty Rynne felt her jittery unease beginning to recede, leaving her with stark astonishment. She knew Nuala well. She'd known her since they were six, when first they'd been at school together. There had never been any sign whatsoever of stuff like this: Nuala was what she looked like, down-to-earth and sensible, both feet on the ground.

'The pregnancy? Would it be that, Nuala?'

'It's no different from the others. It's just that I thought of the way things are with you. And with Corry, talking about going to work on the roads.'

Two troubles, Etty Rynne heard then, and something good drawn out of them when you'd put them together. That's all it was, Nuala said; no more than that.

'What you said will never go outside these four walls,' Etty Rynne promised. 'Nor mentioned within them either.' It was a woman's thing, whatever it was. Wild horses wouldn't drag the conversation they'd had out of her. 'Didn't you mean well? Don't I know you did?'

The coffee calmed their two different moods. They walked through the narrow hall together and a cold breeze blew in when the front door was opened. A car drew up at the petrol pumps and Etty Rynne hurried to attend to it. She waved when Nuala rode away from the crossroads on the bicycle she shared with her husband.

*

'It's how it is,' Corry said when he rejected O'Flynn's offer of a place in the stoneyard, and he said it again when he agreed to work on the roads.

Stubbornly, Nuala considered that it needn't be how it was. It was ridiculous that there should live within a mile of one another a barren wife and a statue-maker robbed by adverse circumstances of his purpose in God's world. It was stupid and silly and perverse, when all that had to be done was to take savings out of a bank. The buttercup-yellow room so lovingly prepared would never now be occupied. In the tarmac surfaces he laid on roads Corry would see the visions he had betrayed.

Nuala nursed her anger, keeping it to herself. She went about her tasks, collecting eggs from where her hens had laid, preparing food, kneading dough for the bread she made every second day; and all the time her anger nagged. It surely was not too terrible a sin, too redolent of insidious presumption, that people should impose an order of their own on what they were given? Had she been clumsy in her manner of putting it to Etty Rynne? Or wrong not to have revealed her intentions to Corry in the hope that, with thought, he would have accepted the sense of them? But doubt spread then: Corry never would have; no matter how it had been put, Etty Rynne would have been terrified.

Corry bought new boots before he went to work on the roads. They were doing a job on the quarry boreen, he said, re-surfacing it because of the complaints there'd been from the lorry drivers. A protective cape was supplied to him in case there'd be rain.

On the night before his new work began Nuala watched him applying waterproof stuff to the boots and rubbing it in. They were useless without it, he'd been told. He took it all in his stride.

'Things happen differently,' he said, as if something in Nuala's demeanour allowed him to sense her melancholy. 'We're never in charge.'

She didn't argue; there was no point in argument. She might have confessed instead that she had frightened Etty Rynne; she might have tried to explain that her wild talk had been an effort to make something good out of what there was, as so often she had seen the spread of angels' wings emerging from roughly sawn wood. But all that was too difficult, so Nuala said nothing.

Her anger was still merciless when that day ended; and through the dark of the night she felt herself oppressed by it and bleakly prayed, waiting for a response that did not come. She reached out in the morning dusk to hold for a moment her husband's hand. Had he woken she would have told him all she had kept to herself, unable now to be silent.

But it was Corry's day that was beginning, and it was he who needed sympathy and support. Making breakfast for him and for her children, Nuala gave him both as best she could, banishing from her mood all outward traces of what she knew would always now be private. When the house was empty again but for herself, she washed up the morning's dishes and tidied the kitchen as she liked to have it. She damped the fire down in the stove. Outside, she fed her hens.

In Corry's workshop she remained longer than she usually did on her morning visit to the saints who had become her friends: St Laurence with his gridiron, St Gabriel the messenger, St Clare of Assisi, St Thomas the Apostle and blind St Lucy, St Catherine, St Agnes. Corry had made them live for her and she felt the first faint slipping away of her anger as they returned her gaze with undisturbed tranquillity. Touched by it, lost in its peace, she sensed their resignation too. The world, not she, had failed.

Rose Wept

'How nice all this is!' Rose's mother cried, with dishes on the way to the dinner table Rose had laid. 'What weather, Mr Bouverie, don't you think? Please sit here next to me.'

Obediently Mr Bouverie did so, replying to the comment about the weather.

'Can't stand a heatwave,' Mr Dakin cheerfully grumbled.

Rose's father – Mrs Dakin's better half, so she insisted – was bluff and genial. He spoke with a hoarseness, always keeping his voice down as if saving it for professional use, he being an auctioneer. Apart from her shrillness, there was a similarity about his wife: both were large and shared an ease often to be found in people of their girth and stature. This evening Mr Dakin was sweating, as he tended to in summer; he had taken his jacket off and undone the buttons of the waistcoat he always wore no matter what the temperature.

His daughter sweltered in her guilt. Rose was eighteen and wished, this evening, she could be somewhere else. She wished she didn't have to meet Mr Bouverie's weary eyes or watch him being polite, listening with inclined head to her mother, smiling at her father's bonhomie. The occasion was a celebration: Rose was to go to university, Mr Bouverie had had a hand in her success. As a tutor, he had made borderline cases his business for more than thirty years, but intended to no longer, Rose being his last. *My God, this is appalling*, she thought. She had begged her mother not to issue this invitation but Mrs Dakin had insisted that they must. Mr Bouverie had attempted to refuse but had then been offered a choice of evenings.

'How I adore the asparagus season!' Rose heard her mother cry in her vivacious way, pressing a dish of the vegetable, well buttered, on their visitor.

Mr Bouverie smiled and murmured his appreciation. He was a man of sixty-odd. Strands of faded hair were hardly noticeable on the freckled pate of his head. There were freckles, also, on the backs of his hands, on old worn skin like dried-out chamois. He wore a pale suit and one of his colourful Italian bow ties.

'And how is your world, Mr Bouverie?' Mr Dakin civilly enquired.

'Shrinking,' Mr Bouverie replied. 'That is something you notice as you age.'

Mrs Dakin bubbled into good-sort laughter. Mr Dakin poured claret.

'You shrink yourself of course.' Mr Bouverie obligingly pursued the subject, since it was clear that the Dakins liked to have a conversation going. He smiled at Rose. Half his teeth were still his own, grey and sucked away to crags.

'Good tidings for the obese,' mumbled Mr Dakin, his features screwed up as they often were when he made a joke. Directed against himself, his banter caused his wife to exclaim:

'Oh, Bobo, you're not obese!'

'I used to be six foot and half an inch,' Mr Bouverie laboured on. 'I'm nothing like that now.'

'But otherwise all is well?' Mr Dakin enquired.

'Oh, yes, indeed.'

Mrs Dakin had had her dining-room papered blue, a dark stripe and a lighter one. Curtains matched, the paintwork was white. Mrs Dakin enjoyed this side of things and often said so: leafless delphiniums patterned her drawing-room; her hall and staircase were black and gold.

'I say, this is awfully good.' Mr Dakin complimented his wife on what she had done with the turkey slices that accompanied the asparagus.

'Delicious,' Mr Bouverie affirmed.

Rose wore a slate-grey dress, with a collar that folded back. Unlike her parents, Rose was petite, her fair hair cut short, a fringe following the curve of her forehead, her eyes a forget-me-not shade of blue. Her guilt, this evening, silenced her, and her smile came fleetingly and not often. When it did, her lower lip lost its bee-sting look and for an instant her white, irregular teeth appeared. She felt awkward and unpretty at the dinner table, sick of herself.

'We cultivate it late in our garden,' her mother was

saying, still talking about the asparagus, of which Rose had taken only a single shoot. 'Our season runs almost to September.'

What kind of an ordeal was it for him? Rose wondered. They had invited his wife as well but a message had come the day before to say that Mrs Bouverie was unwell. Rose knew that wasn't true. His wife had seized the opportunity; she'd said to him she couldn't be bothered, but that wasn't true either. His wife would be naked now, Rose thought.

'Extraordinary, what you read on cars' rear windows,' her mother suddenly remarked, the subject of a particular season for asparagus now exhausted. '*Baby on Board*, for instance. I mean, why on earth should a total stranger be interested in that?'

'I think you're being told not to drive too close,' Rose's father suggested.

Tinkling with unmalicious social laughter, her mother pointed out that it was an enticement to drive too close in order to read what was said.

'They haven't thought of that, my dear.'

In all her chosen subjects Rose had been a borderline case and every Thursday afternoon, for almost a year, had gone to Mr Bouverie's house, where they had sat together in the bow window that looked out into the garden. Mrs Bouverie brought tea as soon as Rose arrived and while they drank it Mr Bouverie didn't attempt to teach but instead talked about the past, about his own life when he had been about to go to university himself, and later being interviewed for a position in the worsted-cloth business. He had tried the worsted trade for a while and then had turned to schoolmastering. But something about the form of discipline and the tedium of 'hobbies time' – when the boys put together model aeroplanes – caused him to give it up after a year. Ever since, he had received pupils in his house, deciding only a month or so ago that Rose should be the last of them. 'Anno Domini,' he'd said, but Rose knew that wasn't the reason. During all those teatimes he had spun his life out, like a serial story.

'But it's odd,' Mrs Dakin lightly persisted. 'Don't you agree with me, Mr Bouverie?'

The old man hesitated, and Rose could see he had momentarily lost track of the conversation. She knew her mother would notice also and not be dismayed. Smoothly her mother said:

'All those personal declarations on motor cars – whom people love, where they've been, who occupies the two front seats.'

'Sharon and Liam usually,' Mr Dakin guffawed.

Mrs Bouverie, ten years younger than her husband and seeming more, had a lover. Mrs Bouverie, slim and silky, with long legs and a wrinkled pout, too well made up, received a visitor on Thursday afternoons because her husband was occupied with the last of his pupils then, concentrating on a borderline case's weaknesses. Mrs Bouverie's visitor came softly, but there were half-muffled sounds, like shadows passing through the house, a pattern of whispers and footfalls, a gently closed door, and always – ten minutes or so before Rose was due to leave the house herself – the lightest of footsteps on the stairs and in the hall. It was a pattern that belonged with Mrs Bouverie's placing the tea tray on the pale mahogany of the window table, her scent lingering after she left the room, the restlessness in her eyes. But Rose hadn't entirely guessed the nature of the weekly rendezvous until the afternoon she went to fetch a handkerchief from her coat pocket on the hallstand, and saw a sallow-faced man with a latchkey in his hand breathlessly closing the hall door. Seeing her in turn, he smiled, a brightly secret smile. 'Younger than her?' Rose's friend Caroline, sharp on detail, wanted to know, and Rose said no, not much, but beautifully turned out in a brown linen suit, a grey-haired man, and elegant. 'Not come to mend something?' suggested Daisy, who could not help being sceptical when someone else claimed the limelight. Her doubts were scorned at once by Angela and Liz, for why should a repairer of washing machines or television sets be in possession of a latchkey and be dressed so? Why should he come so regularly? Why should he smile a secret smile? In the Box Tree Café where the five girls gossiped and complained of this and that, where they talked about sex and other private matters, where Daisy and Caroline smoked, Mrs Bouverie's Thursday lover became the subject of intense and specific speculation.

He was married, Caroline said, which was why he had to come to her house: in illicit love affairs there was always the difficulty of finding somewhere to go. He came on Thursdays because, Rose being the last of Mr Bouverie's pupils, there was no other time when Mr Bouverie was fully occupied as perhaps there had been in the past, when there were other pupils. 'That kind of thing and she's *fifty*?' Daisy frowned through the words, but Angela said fifty was nothing. 'I do not intend to be unfaithful,' Liz romantically declared, but the others weren't interested in that, any more than they wished to dwell for long on the advanced age of Mrs Bouverie. What fascinated all of them, Daisy too in the end, was that while Rose sat in a room that had been described to them – a long low-ceilinged room that had once been two, with sofas and arm-chairs and a circular mirror over the mantelpiece – in a room upstairs a man and a woman got into bed together. 'I would love to see him,' Caroline said. 'Even a glance.' Was it like, each of them wondered in the Box Tree Café, the lovemaking you saw on the tele-vision or in the cinema? Or was, somehow, the real thing quite different? They argued about that. 'I would not hesitate to be unfaithful,' Caroline said, 'if things went stale.' Caroline was like that, her matter-of-factness sometimes sounding hard. Angela – long black hair, brown eyes, rarely smiling because of her dental wires – was the victim kind, and accident-prone. Liz gave too much, generosity part of her romantic nature.

Daisy, red-haired and bespectacled, distrusted the world. Liz was the prettiest of the five, with neat features and flaxen hair in a ponytail and a film star's mouth, nothing particularly special except for deep-blue eyes, but still the prettiest. Rose thought of herself as ordinary, too quiet, too shy and nervous: Mrs Bouverie and her Thursday visitor were a godsend in her relationship with her friends.

'How nice all this is!' Mrs Dakin enthused for the second time, the subject of notices on motor cars having run its course. 'How hugely grateful to you we are, Mr Bouverie!'

Rose watched him shaking his head, and heard him saying that the credit must wholly go to her.

'No, truly, Mr Bouverie,' her father insisted with a solemn intonation.

'All her young life before her,' her mother threw in.

Rose hadn't told them, nor told her brother. It wasn't the sort of thing that was talked about within this family. She would have been embarrassed and would have caused embarrassment – a very different reception from the one there'd been when she had passed the information on in the Box Tree Café with its green-topped tables. After the first time, her friends had always been expectant. 'It could be any of our mothers,' Liz whispered, awestruck, once. They had sat there, coffee drunk, Caroline and Daisy with their cigarettes, dwelling upon that, imagining Rose's sallow-skinned man arriving in the surroundings that had been described to them. 'Beautifully pressed, his linen suit,' Rose said. 'And a plain green shirt.'

Around the dinner table the conversation, still powered by Mrs Dakin, had changed again. '*The Kindest Cut*,' she was saying now, drawing Mr Bouverie's attention to the droll wit of hairdressers as exemplified in the titles chosen for their premises. '*Nutters* I saw the other day!'

This evening, for the very last time, he would be there. Mr Bouverie did not normally go out to dinner; he'd said as much when joining in the celebratory mood on his arrival. No tea tray had been carried to the window table since Rose had ceased to visit the house. The invitation for this evening must have seemed like a gift, naughtily wrapped, for slim Mrs Bouverie. 'It's a Mr Azam,' her husband had said on the last but one of their Thursdays. 'In case you are interested in his name.'

Mr Dakin poured the wine again. He said they'd had the glasses as a wedding present, only four of them left so they couldn't use them often.

'The Mitages,' Mrs Dakin murmured softly, the shrillness that whistled through her voice gone from it now, inappropriate because the Mitages were no longer alive. She paused in her eating, inclining her head in memory, slanting it a little to the left, a wistful smile enlivening her reddened lips. Mr Dakin sighed; then death passed on, and Mrs Dakin picked up her fork again and the wine bottle was replaced on its little silver tray, another wedding gift, although this was not said.

'Cuckold.' In the Box Tree Café the ugly word, spoken first by Caroline, had formed in their minds, its sound acquiring shape and colour. Only Rose knew what Mr Bouverie looked like but he, really, scarcely came into it. It was not an old man who had once planned a future in the cloth trade and had ended as a tutor that was of interest. He was no rival for the darkened bedroom above the room that had once been two, or for the scent of Mrs Bouverie or her lover's suit draped on a chair, or smears of lipstick left on sallow flesh. No one ever interposed a comment while Rose spread out for the delectation of her friends another Thursday harvest. Once, music softly played, 'Smoke Gets in Your Eyes'. Once the telephone rang and was not answered by Mr Bouverie, although the receiver was only yards from where they sat. Sooner than if he had crossed to it the ringing ceased, answered at the bedside. Not always, but now and again, Mrs Bouverie appeared on the stairs when Rose was putting her coat on at the hallstand; or in summer, when there was no coat, she sometimes called down goodbye when she heard the voices of her husband and his pupil. 'Vicious,' Liz said. 'That's a vicious woman.' But Rose said no, you couldn't call Mrs Bouverie vicious; she didn't strike you as that. 'More significant that she's childless,' Daisy said. 'Or at least it could be.' Caroline disagreed.

'Oh, my golly gosh!' Rose's father exclaimed with his auctioneer's jolliness when gooseberry fool was placed in front of him. Mrs Dakin said the gooseberries had been picked from her own bushes.

'Delicious,' Mr Bouverie for the second time re-marked, and the talk was of gooseberries for a while, of different varieties, one favoured for this purpose, another for that.

'Mr Azam,' Rose had announced in the Box Tree Café and Daisy had gone at once to the telephone directory to look the name up. 'Hundreds,' she'd said, returning. 'Hundreds of Azams.' In her absence the conversation had advanced in another direction, the name agreed to be a foreign one and then abandoned as a subject for discussion. 'When a husband knows,' Caroline said, 'he's not so much a cuckold as com-plaisant.' And they talked about the fact that while Mr Bouverie dealt with the last of his borderline cases he knew what was occurring all around him – the nature of the creaking stairs and closing doors, the light tap of footsteps not his wife's, the snatch of music hushed. 'Did he seem different when he said the name?' Caroline sharply asked, and Rose said no.

Her brother Jason arrived. Like his parents, he was well covered, with a jowl that was identically his father's and with his mother's small fat hands, bland in his manner. It was because of Jason that Mr Bouverie had been discovered, for Jason in his time had been a borderline case also. They greeted one another now, shaking hands and enquiring about one another's well being.

'How did it do?' Jason asked Mr Dakin when all that was over.

'Oh, well enough. The Chippendale fetched a price. A happy day's business,' Mr Dakin reported, smiling.

'How very nice!' His wife glanced round the table, seeking to share her exultation in the day's success. 'All right, dear?' she asked when her gaze lighted on her daughter. 'All right, Rose?'

Rose nodded, lying. 'I do mind, as a matter of fact,' he had said, as if he knew all about the Box Tree Café and the audience of five crowding the same green-topped corner table, as if he had listened to every word. Guilt had come then, beginning in that moment. His spectacles had slipped to one side and he adjusted them as soon as he had spoken. The cuffs of his blue tweed jacket were trimmed with leather. 'Yes,' she'd said, not knowing what else to say, the waves of guilt already a sickness in her stomach. 'Yes.' It was as though for all the months that had passed they, too, had shared a secret, the secret of knowing everything that was happening and not saying. When her Thursday visits came to an end a way of life would finish for him also, for Rose knew that Mr Azam would not just come to the house and march upstairs while the old cuckold sighed and blinked. That would not be: all of it had to do with pretence, and deception of a kind. 'I'm sorry,' she had wanted to say, and did not know why she would have given anything not to have blurted out so much in the Box Tree Café. She had longed to share his confidences with him, but had betrayed him even before he offered them.

In the lovers' bedroom Rose saw Mrs Bouverie close her eyes in ecstasy, while the gooseberry fool was finished and Jason spoke of a function he had attended, how one man had gone on and on. Coffee came and was poured at the table. 'Don't go yet. Oh, love, don't go,' Mrs Bouverie pleaded, and Mr Azam said he didn't ever want to go.

Across the table, all that was in Mr Bouverie's face, as so much had been when he gave the man a name and later when he said he minded. It was there behind the spectacles, in the tired skin touched with two crimson wine-blurs above the cheekbones. They shared it, yet they did not. Their sharing was a comfort for him, yet the comfort was as false as his wife's voice on the stairs.

'All right, dear?' her mother asked again, and by way of response Rose reached out for her coffee.

A frown began to knit Mr Dakin's forehead. Jason coughed and touched his face with a handkerchief, then folded it into his top pocket and began again about the function he had attended, referring to a commercial prospect he had advanced. His father nodded, thankfully diverted. Mrs Dakin tidied the surface up, murmuring to Mr Bouverie that probably he'd never guess she'd been shy herself at Rose's age.

'I'm confident we'll pick it up,' Jason said. 'I'll write tomorrow, see if we can't clinch.'

Mrs Bouverie clung to her lover, saying no this couldn't be the last time, sobbing over him, noisily exclaiming that something better was their due. But Mr Azam only shook his head. He was not a man to cause a wife who had borne his children to suffer. 'We have our dignity, you and I,' he said. 'We have been given this much.' Mr Azam drew on his green shirt, and brushed his hair with a hairbrush on the dressing-table, and saw that the lipstick smears were gone. 'I saw the pupil once,' he said, but the woman he spoke to had turned her face to the wall.

'Sounds promising,' Mr Dakin complimented Jason. 'Sure to work out, I'd say.'

Mrs Dakin poured more coffee. She spoke of names, how it had struck her this afternoon that names can inspire the quality they suggest. She described a Prudence she had known when she was Rose's age, and a Verity. 'Remember Ernest Calavor?' she prompted Mr Dakin, and he said yes indeed. Bitter chocolates were passed round in a slim red box. When she'd refused one Rose offered it across the table to Mr Bouverie.

'Thank you, Rose.'

The lover's footsteps were on the stairs, and then the front door closed and he was gone.

'It's been so good of you,' Mr Bouverie said. 'So very kind of you to have me.'

'I hope your wife,' Mrs Dakin began.

'She was so sorry to miss an evening out.'

'There'll be another time. We'll keep in touch.'

'Always good to see you,' Mr Dakin added. 'Cheers us no end.'

The old man hesitated before he rose to go. Had he not done so Rose might not have wept. But Mr Bouverie hesitated and Rose wept to exclamations of concern, and fuss and embarrassment, while Mr Bouverie stood awkwardly. She wept for his silent suffering, for his having to accept a distressing invitation because of her mother's innocent insistence. She wept for the last golden opportunity the occasion provided for two other people, for the woman whose sinning caused her in the end to turn her face to the wall, for the man whom duty bound to a wife. She wept for the *modus vivendi* that was left in the house no pupil or lover would visit again, for the glimpse she had had of it, enough to allow her a betrayal. She wept for her friends – for the unfaithful when things turned stale, and for the accident-prone; for the romantic, who gave too much, and the mistrustful. She wept for the brittle surface of her mother's good-sort laughter and her father's jolliness, and Jason settling into a niche. She wept for all her young life before her, and other glimpses and other betrayals.

Big Bucks

Fina waited on the pier, watching the four men dragging the boat on the shingle. She watched while the catch was landed and some damage to the nets examined. At the top of the steps that brought them near to where she stood the men parted and she went to John Michael.

'Your mother,' Fina said, and she watched him guessing that his mother was dead now. 'I'm sorry, John Michael,' she said. 'I'm sorry.'

He nodded, silent, as she knew he would be. It was cold and darkening as they walked together to the cottage where his mother was. Grey on grey, swiftly blown clouds threatened rain. They could go now, Fina's thought was. They could make a life for themselves.

'Father Clery was there,' she said.

*

'Have you plans?' John Michael's uncle – his mother's brother – enquired after the funeral. Plans were necessary: John Michael's father had drowned when John Michael was an infant, his fisherman's cottage then becoming his widow's by right for her lifetime. In a different arrangement – John Michael being a fisherman himself – a cottage would become his in time, but not yet, he being the youngest, the only young one among older men.

'I'll go,' he said in reply to his uncle's question.

Fina heard that said, the confirmation given that John Michael had been waiting only for the death. Going was a tradition, time-honoured, the chance of it coming in different ways, the decision long dwelt upon before it was taken. Bat Quinn – who had stayed – had a way of regretfully pointing over the sea to the horizon beyond the two rocks that were islands in the bay. 'Big bucks,' he'd say, and name the men of his own generation who had gone in search of them: Donoghue and Artie Hiney and Meagher and Flynn, and Big Reilly and Matt Cready. There were others who'd gone inland or to England, but they hadn't done as well.

'A thing I'll put to you,' John Michael's uncle was saying now, 'is the consideration of the farm.'

'The farm?'

'When I'm buried myself.'

'What about the farm?'

'I'm saying it'll be left.'

Still listening, Fina heard a statement made through what was being left out: the farm would pass to John Michael, since there was no one else to inherit it.

'I get a tiredness those days,' John Michael's uncle said. His wasted features and old man's bloodshot eyes confirmed this revelation. Two years ago he'd been widowed; after a childless marriage he was alone.

'There's a while in you yet,' John Michael said.

'I can't manage the acres.'

They could be on the farm already was what was being suggested, and it wouldn't be hard to pull the place together. Inland from the sea, where the air was softer and you didn't live in fear of what the sea would take from you, they could make a life there. The heart had gone from the old man, but he wasn't difficult. He wouldn't be a burden in the time that was left to him.

'Ah, no, no.' John Michael shook his head, his rejection not acknowledging in any other way what was being offered. America was what he and Fina wanted, what they'd always talked about. That evening John Michael said he had the fare saved.

*

The plans that could not be made in the lifetime of John Michael's mother were made now. John Michael would go soon. In May he would return for the wedding, and take Fina back with him. He didn't know what work he'd get, but according to Bat Quinn it had never mattered to the men who'd gone before that fishing was all they knew. 'Leave it open till you'll get there, boy,' Bat Quinn advised, the same advice he had been giving for forty years. Matt Cready came back, the only one who did, his big bucks spent like pennies every night in the bar of the half-and-half. 'Look at that, boy,' Bat Quinn invited, displaying for John Michael the dollar bill he kept in an inside pocket. Bat Quinn had a niece, a nun in Delaware, and had had a sister in Chicago until her death two years ago. Slouched heavily at the bar of the grocery and public house that Fina's family kept, his great paunch straining his clothes, his small eyes watery from drink, Bat Quinn showed everyone his dollar. 'I'll send you back another,' John Michael always promised, and Fina always giggled.

They knew one another well, had gone together to school, picked up on the pier every morning by the bus, the only two from the village at that time. Concerned about the adventure that was being embarked upon, Fina's father had protested more than once that they were still no more than the children they'd been then. 'Oh, John Michael'll fall on his feet,' her mother predicted, fond of John Michael, optimistic on his behalf. 'But isn't he welcome to move in with us all the same?' Fina's father had offered when John Michael's mother died, and Fina passed that on, knowing that John Michael wouldn't ever consider serving in the half-and-half, drawing pints or checking the shelves for which grocery items were running out.

'Sure, we have to go,' was all John Michael said himself. Fina's own two brothers had gone, one to Dublin, the other to England. One or other of them would have had the inheritance of the half-and-half but both had turned their backs on it.

A few evenings before they were to be parted, they walked through the twilight on the strand, talking about what they intended to reject for ever: the sea and the fishing, or John Michael being beholden in the half-and-half, his uncle's farm. Eleven miles away, beyond the town of Kinard – which had a minimarket, a draper's, five public houses, a hardware, and Power's Medical Hall – the farmhouse was remote, built without foundations according to John Michael. Slated and whitewashed, it was solitary where it stood except for the yard sheds, its four fields stretching out behind it, as far as the boglands that began with the slope of the mountain. The mountain had no name, John Michael said, or if it had it was forgotten now, and there wasn't a gate that swung. Old bedsteads blocked the holes in the hedges, there was a taste of turf on the water you drank. Damp brought on mildew in the rooms.

'Even if you could get the place up on its feet again,' John Michael said, 'it's never what we want.'

'No way.' Vehemently Fina shook her head, reassurance and agreement bright in her eyes. 'No way,' she said again.

Physically, there was a similarity about them, both of them slightly made, John Michael hardly a head taller. Both were dark-haired, with a modesty in their features, as there was in their manner. They seemed more vulnerable when they were together than when they were on their own.

'Did you ever think it, though, Fina? That we'd be on our way?'

Her hand was warm in his, and his felt strong, although she knew it wasn't particularly. Since they were children they had belonged to one another. On this same strand two years ago, in the twilight of an evening also, they had first spoken of love.

'I only wish I'd be going with you,' she said now.

'Ah sure, it's not long.'

*

He was gone, quite suddenly. For two hundred and one days they would be parted: already Fina had counted them. She thought at first that maybe at the last moment he'd be sent back, that the immigration-control men at Shannon wouldn't let him on to the plane because he didn't possess a work permit. But he'd said he'd be ready for that and he must have been. You had to be up to the tricks, he'd said.

The first day without him passed and when it was the evening of the next one Bat Quinn was talking about big bucks again, his small eyes squinting at Fina from the red fat of his face. Only Jamesie O'Connor was ever sent back, he said, on account of his dead leg. 'Don't worry, girl,' Bat Quinn consoled, and began about the schooner that was pitched up on the rocks when he was five years old, twelve foreign men taken in for burial. 'Sure, what's here for John Michael only the like of that? And isn't he safe with the mighty dollar to watch over him?' Bat Quinn had more talk in him than anyone who ever came into the half-and-half. If exile or shipwrecks weren't his subject it would be the Corpus Christi he had walked to in his childhood, twenty-three miles to Kinard, twenty-three miles back again, or how an old priest used to bless the hurley sticks of the team he favoured, or the firing of Lisreagh House. Bat Quinn had been a fisherman himself, going out with the boats for more than fifty years. He'd never worn a collar or tie in his life, he shaved himself once a week and had never had the need of a wife; he washed his clothes when they required it. All that Bat Quinn would tell you, having told you most of it before. He had stayed at home when the others went, but even so he insisted that Boston's long, straight streets were a wonder when the evening sun shone down them. You'd go into McDaid's and there was shamrock in pots and a photo of Christy Ring. He had it as a fact that Donoghue got to be a candy king before he went to his grave in a green-upholstered coffin. Artie Hiney made his stack in the wheatfields of Kansas. Big Reilly rose high in the Frisco police force and ran it in the end.

I missed you the minute I left, John Michael wrote. There was a lot to tell her, his first letter went on, but even so it was short. He wasn't used to writing letters, he'd said before he went away, he'd do his best. *I have work with a gang*, he wrote when three weeks had gone by, and unable to help herself Fina thought of gangsters.

She laughed, as though John Michael were there to laugh with her.

There were tourists here last week, she wrote herself.
*Italian people who asked Mary Doleen would there be fish
today. They came into the shop and we thought they were
German but they said Italian. They'd be back for fish in the
morning, they said, but they never came. Bat Quinn was on
the pier waiting, wanting to know was it Rome they were
from. There were never Italians here before, he said, the time
of the wreck it was Spaniards washed up. He was down on
the pier the next few mornings, but they never came back.*

John Michael replied directly to that, saying he was working with an Italian but he didn't know his name. It was labouring work, he said. 'Give him time, girl,' Bat Quinn advised, but when more weeks went by there was no mention of the streets of Boston or the Kansas wheatlands. Then a letter came that asked Fina not to write because there wouldn't be an address to write to for a while. John Michael said he'd let her know when he had one again.

In this way Fina and John Michael began to lose touch. You had to lodge where you could, John Michael had explained; you wouldn't earn a penny if you paid regular rent. Fina didn't entirely understand this. She couldn't see that you could lodge anywhere without paying rent, and it was too late now to ask. John Michael had to take what he could get, she of course could see that. He had to move about if it was the only way; if he said so it must be right.

A cold, sunny November began, but the pattern of the days themselves didn't change much. Fina served in the shop, slicing rashers on the machine, adding up bills, unpacking the items that were delivered – the jams and meat pastes and tinned goods, the porridge meal and dried goods, the baking ingredients in their bulky cartons. O'Brien's bread van brought the bread from Kinard on Tuesdays and Fridays, milk came on alternate days and there was the longlife if it was held up, which sometimes it was. Experience had taught the family of the half-and-half the business, what to order and when, what to keep in stock both in the shop and in the bar. You could be caught out if you didn't know what you were doing, Fina's mother used to say; you could have stuff on the shelves for a generation or find yourself running out because you hadn't looked ahead. Her mother ran the shop and took a rest in the evenings when the men came into the bar and Fina's father was in charge. Her mother was as lightly made as Fina was, small and busy, with a certain knowledge of where everything was on the crowded shelves of the grocery, quick with figures, spectacles suspended on a chain. Fina's father – assisted in the bar by Fina, as her mother was in the shop – was a big man, slow of movement and thought, silver-haired, always in his shirtsleeves, the sleeves themselves rolled up. He put on a black suit to go to Mass, and a tie with a tiepin, and wore a hat for the walk through the village. Fina's mother dressed herself carefully also, in a coat and hat that were not otherwise worn. The three of them went together on Sundays and separately at other times, to confession or confraternity.

John Michael didn't write when he had no address, and Fina fell back on her imagination. The world of America, which she and John Michael had talked about and wondered about for so long, was spiced with the yarns of Bat Quinn, his exaggeration and fantasy steadied by facts remembered from the days when Mr Horan unrolled the map of the continent and hung it on the blackboard. On the glossy surface the states were shown in shades of brown and green and yellow, the Great Lakes blue. Iron came from Minnesota and Michigan and Pennsylvania, uranium from Colorado. Cotton and tobacco belonged to the south.

The tip of Mr Horan's cane moved in a straight line, horizontally, up and down, dividing Nebraska from South Dakota, Oregon from Idaho. It rapped the dates of admission to the Union, it traced the course of the long Mississippi, it touched the Rockies. You listened because you had to, stifling yawns of tedium, thankfully forgetting what the Louisiana Purchase was. The scissor-tailed flycatcher was the state bird of Oklahoma, the peony was the flower of Indiana. It was in Milwaukee that Donoghue became a candy king.

The tattered schoolroom cane picking out the facts had failed to create much of a reality. Bat Quinn's

second-hand information didn't inspire Fina as it did
John Michael. But America lived for both of them on
the screen high up above the bar of the half-and-half or
the one in John Michael's kitchen. For two years before
she died his mother had to be helped to go to bed and
as often as she could Fina assisted. Afterwards she sat
with John Michael in the kitchen, with tea and pink
Mikado biscuits and the sound turned low. They
watched America, they heard its voices. Its ballgame
heroes battled, rigid in their padding and their helmets.
Steam swirled above the night-time gratings of its city
streets. Legs wide, eyes dead, its gangsters splayed their
fingers on precinct walls.

Fina liked it when the doormen greeted the yellow
cabs, and the quick talk in the skyscraper lifts, and
Christmas in the stores. She liked the lone driver on
the highway, music on his radio, the wayside gas station
he drew up at, its attendant swatting flies. She liked the
boy who drilled for oil too near the old-time ranch,
everything changing because the gush of oil was what
mattered now, the boy in the end a bigtime millionaire.
College days, Thanksgiving, Robert E. Lee: she liked
all that. 'You want to?' John Michael would whisper
and Fina always nodded, never hesitating.

I got work in a laundry, the next letter said, slow in
coming. Bat Quinn wagged his head in admiration
when he heard. There were big bucks in the laundry
business, no doubt about it. The President's shirts
would have to go to a laundry, and Bat Quinn twisted

round on his barstool, exclaiming loudly that John Michael Gallagher was in charge of the shirts of the President of the United States. 'I'll tell you a thing, girl, you hit it lucky with John Michael Gallagher.'

Fina put all that in a letter, making a joke of it, as they would have in the past. It was a long letter, with bits of news saved up from the period when they'd been out of touch: O'Brien's bread van breaking down, the boats unable to go out for four days, the widow dancing at Martin Shaul's wake. She wondered if John Michael had an accent now, like Bat Quinn said Matt Cready acquired.

A Christmas card came in January and a fortnight later a letter with an address, 2a Beaver Street, a room that was big enough for both of them. *I painted it out,* John Michael wrote. *I cleaned the windows.* Ninety-one days had passed and the ones that were passing now had begun to lengthen. In Kinard a week ago Fina had chosen the material for her dress. She kept telling herself it wouldn't be all that long before the first banns were called.

The morning the letter about the room came there was an iciness in the air when she walked on the strand, thinking about the banns and thinking about Beaver Street. She imagined a fire escape zig-zagging on an outside wall, a big metal structure she had seen in a film, windows opening on to it. She imagined a poor neighbourhood because that was what John Michael could afford, spindly trees struggling to grow along a sidewalk. She wouldn't object to a poor neighbour-hood, she knew he'd done his best.

The strand was empty that morning. The fishing boats were still out, there had been no one on the pier when she went by it. New shells were embedded in the clean, damp sand where she walked, washed by the waves that lapped softly over them. Once upon a time, so the story was told in the village, a woman had walked all the way to Galway, going after the man she loved. Missing John Michael more than ever, even though the time was shortening with every day, Fina understood that now. Slowly, she made her way back to the village, the room he had found for them more vivid in her consciousness than anything she saw.

*

She knew when her father called her. She had heard the ringing of the telephone above the clatter of voices in the bar, and her father's surprise when he responded. 'Well, b'the holy farmer! How are you at all?' She pushed the glass she'd just filled across the counter. 'Wait'll I get Fina for you,' she heard her father say, and when she picked the receiver up John Michael's voice was there at once.

'Hullo, Fina.'

He didn't sound distant, only unusual, because in all the time of their friendship they had never spoken on the telephone to one another.

'John Michael!'

'Did you get my letter, Fina? About the room?'

'I got it yesterday.'

'Are you OK, Fina?'

'Oh, I am, I am. Are you, yourself?' There wouldn't be telephone calls, he'd said before he went, and she agreed: telephone calls would eat up what he earned. But hearing his voice was worth every penny they'd lose.

'I'm good, Fina.'

'It's great to hear you.'

'Listen, Fina, there's a thing we have to think about.' He paused for a second or two. 'A difficulty about May, Fina.'

'Difficulty?'

'About coming back.'

He paused again, and then he had to repeat some of what he said because she couldn't follow it. It was why he had phoned. Because he knew it would sound complicated, but actually it wasn't: it was best he didn't come back in May for the wedding. It was best because once you'd got to where he was now, once you'd got into steady work, it wasn't easy to come and go. He shouldn't be working at all, he said. Like hawks, he said they were.

'You understand, Fina?'

She nodded in the darkened shop, where the telephone was. There was a smell of bacon, and of stout and spirits drifting in from the other side of the half-and-half.

The deep-freeze began to sound, registering its periodic intake of electricity. *Chef Soups*, a point-of-sale inducement read, close enough to discern, the rest of its message lost in the gloom.

'If I was to come over I wouldn't get back in again.'

It would be better to be married in America. It would be better if she came over and he stayed where he was. He asked her if she understood and she felt as if she were stumbling about, in some kind of a dream without sense in it, but even so she said she understood.

'I think of you all the time, John Michael. I love you.'

'It's the same way with me. We'll work something out. Only it's different than we thought.'

'Different?'

'All the time you're thinking would you be sent back.'

'We'll be married in America, John Michael.'

'I think of you too, Fina. I love you too.'

They would work something out, he said again, and then there was the click of the receiver replaced. Fina wondered where he was, in what kind of room, and if he was still standing as she was, beside the telephone. Once there had been voices in the background. It would be half past four, still daylight there, and she wondered if he was at work in the laundry and if he'd taken a risk, using the phone like that.

'How's John Michael Gallagher?' Bat Quinn asked, slouched in his corner, on the stool that over the years had become his own. In the dimly illuminated bar the expression on his face was as lost as the words on the Chef point-of-sale had been, but Fina could guess at what was there – the small eyes would be reflecting his excitement because all those miles away John Michael Gallagher had touched success.

'He's doing well, girl. Isn't it grand for the pair of ye?'

By the door of the bar there was a game of twenty-one. The men John Michael had fished with were silent, as they often were. Fina's father washed glasses at the sink.

'He can't come back for the wedding,' Fina said to Bat Quinn. She moved closer to him, drawn to him because with his knowledge of America he would know about the anxiety that was worrying John Michael.

'It's understandable,' Bat Quinn said.

The porter he was drinking was drained away, the glass edged toward her on the scrubbed surface of the bar. Fina refilled it and scooped up the coins that had been counted out.

'It's never as easy as they think,' Bat Quinn said.

Chance had always played a part, ever since the Famine years, that first great exodus from the land, the ships called coffin ships. As often as the good side of it was there, so were misfortune and desperation and failure.

'Never was easy, never will be, girl.'

'Will they take it back?' Fina's mother wondered

about the wedding-dress material. All but the yard she
had begun to cut the arms out of was untouched. Scally
wouldn't return the full price because what was left
would have to be sold as a remnant. You couldn't
expect the full price from a draper like Scally, but
an agreement might be reached to make up for the
disappointment. Fina's mother had sat for a while not
saying anything when she heard the news, and then
she sighed and cheered up, for that was her way. She'd
assumed at first that she'd finish the dress anyway, that
Fina would need it when she married John Michael in
America. But Fina explained it wouldn't be that kind
of wedding now.

'They gave an amnesty a while back,' Fina's father
said. He remembered a figure, something like a hundred and twenty thousand Irish immigrants outside the
system in New York. But it could be a while before
there'd be an amnesty again. 'Go easy now, Fina,' he
advised, not elaborating on that. 'John Michael'll fix
something,' her mother said.

Ten days later John Michael phoned again. He'd
thought more about it, he said; and listening to him,
Fina realized he wasn't just talking about not coming
home for the wedding.

'Don't you want me?' she asked, meaning to add
something to that, to ask if he'd changed his mind
about her coming over. But she left it as she'd said it,
and John Michael reassured her. It was just that he
was wondering would it be too much for them, the

uncertainty there'd be, the hole-in-corner existence; too much for any wife, was what he was wondering. It was all right for some young fellow on his own, who could scuttle around, dodging the bit of trouble. If she was there with him now she'd see what he meant, and Fina imagined that, being with him in the room with the clean windows and the freshly painted walls, all of it ready for her.

'I'll come back,' John Michael said.

'But you said –'

'I'll come back altogether. I'll come back and we'll stay where we are.'

She couldn't say anything. She tried to, but the words kept becoming muddled before she got them out. John Michael said:

'I love you, Fina. Isn't it that that matters? The two of us loving one another?'

It was, she agreed. Of course it was.

'I'll work out the time I'm taken on for.'

They said goodbye. It was a shock for her, he said, and he was sorry. But it was better, no way it wasn't better. Again he said he loved her, and then the line went dead.

It would be his uncle's farm. She guessed that; it hadn't been said. They'd pull the place together; his uncle would stay there with them until he died. John Michael would rather that than going on with the fishing. He'd prefer it to being beholden in the half-and-half.

'There's the odd one comes back all right,' Bat Quinn said, having listened to Fina's side of the telephone conversation.

Fina nodded, not saying anything, and that same week she went out to the farm. She took the Kinard bus and walked the last two miles from where it dropped her off. Sheepdogs barked when she turned in to the yard, but the barking was ignored by John Michael's uncle, as if it didn't matter to him that someone had come, as if all curiosity about visitors had long ago expired. Grass grew through the cobbles, a solitary hen pecked at the edge of a dung pile.

'I was wondering how you were,' Fina said in the kitchen, and the haggard countenance that the farm had defeated was lifted from a perusal of *Ireland's Own*. Boiled potatoes had been tumbled out on to a newspaper, the skins of those eaten in a pile, peas left in a tin. A plate with a knife and fork on it was pushed to one side.

'Sit down, Fina,' the old man invited. 'Wait till I make a cup of tea.'

Life seemed to return to him while he half filled a kettle and put it on a ring of his electric stove. He spooned tea into an unheated pot and set out cups and saucers, and milk in a milking can. He offered bread but Fina shook her head. He took a heel of butter from a safe on the dresser.

'John Michael went over,' he said.

'Yes, he did. A while back.'

'He's settled so.'

'He hasn't the right papers,' Fina said.

She watched while the butter was spread on a slice of bread, and sugar sprinkled over it. It wouldn't take long to set the kitchen to rights. It wouldn't take long to paint over the dingy ceiling, to take up the linoleum from the floor and burn it, to wash every cup and knife and fork, to scrub the grease from the wooden tabletop, to fix the taps that were hanging from the wall, to replace the filthy armchair.

'You were never here before,' the old man said, and led her upstairs to dank bedrooms, an image of Our Lady on the wall opposite each bed. A forgotten cat rushed, hissing, from a windowsill. Electric wire hung crookedly from a fallen-in ceiling, mould was grey on the faded flowers of wallpaper. Downstairs, ivy crept over panes of glass.

A digger would take out those rocks, Fina thought, surveying the fields. Half a day it would take with a digger. John Michael's uncle said they'd be welcome if it was something they'd consider. When the wedding would be over, he said, when they'd have gathered themselves together.

'It's different why you'd go into exile these days,' Bat Quinn said in the half-and-half. 'A different approach you'd have to it.'

You made a choice for yourself now. The way the country was doing well, you could stay where you were or you could travel off. A different thing altogether from the old days, when you had no choice at all.

'Yes,' Fina said.

★

I went over to see the farm, she wrote. *No way we wouldn't be able to get it up and going. He'd be no trouble to us.* Her mother finished the wedding dress. Fina imagined John Michael, any day now, walking in with the red holdall they'd bought together in Kinard. They'd bought her own at the same time, the same colour and size. She imagined going back with him to Scally's and explaining to Scally that they wouldn't want it now. John Michael would be better at that than she'd be.

Fina's feelings bewildered her. She kept hoping that out of the blue the phone would ring and John Michael would say it was all right, that he'd wangled a work permit, that the boss he was working for had put a word in, that there'd been a further amnesty. But then another while would pass and there'd be no hope at all. John Michael would walk in and she'd be shy of him, the way she'd never been. She imagined herself on the farm as she used to imagine herself in the room John Michael had described, the silence of the fields instead of the noise on the streets and the yellow cabs flashing by. When she wondered if she still loved John Michael, she told herself not to be a fool. He was right when he said that it was loving one another that mattered. But then the confusion began again.

No phone call came. *We'll sort things out when I'm back*, another letter said. *We'll have it done before the wedding*. The banns had long ago been called. The half-and-half would be closed for the day. People had been invited to the house. If she had a number, she would telephone herself, Fina thought, not that she'd say anything about how she felt. She woke up in the middle of one night feeling afraid. In the dark she knew she didn't love John Michael.

It's only I'm ruining everything for you, she wrote when there was hardly time for him to receive the letter before he'd have to set out. *I have it on my mind, John Michael*. Alone on the strand, she had decided on that way of putting things. Five days later, two before he was due back, John Michael phoned. He'd got her letter, he said, and then he said he loved her.

'I always will, Fina.'

He could tell: she heard it in his voice. Always quick on the uptake, always receptive of her emotions, even in a letter, even on the long-distance telephone, he knew more than she did herself.

'I don't know what it is,' she said.

'You're uncertain.'

She began to say it wasn't that, but she stumbled and hesitated. She wanted to cry.

'You have to be guided by yourself, Fina. You're doubtful about the wedding.'

She said what she had in her letter, that she was ruining things for him. 'It wouldn't be right to wait until you got here.'

'Better to wait all the same,' he said. 'It's not long.'

'I don't want you to come.'

'You don't love me, Fina?'

He asked that again when she didn't reply.

'I don't know,' she said.

★

John Michael did not come back. For Fina, the pain lasted for the empty weeks that followed the day that had been set for the wedding, and then for all the summer. September was balmy, thirty days of a clear blue sky, the days gently slipping away as they shortened. In October a year had passed since the death of John Michael's mother. By October John Michael's scant letters didn't come any more.

'I'd say he'd walk in in the time ahead,' Bat Quinn said on a night his intake had exceeded what he allowed himself. Squinting blearily up at Fina, he added, as if the two observations somehow belonged together: 'Haven't you the delicate way with you, pouring that stout, girl?'

'Oh, I have all right.'

Bat Quinn was right. It was likely enough that in the time ahead, when John Michael had made his money, he would return, to look about him and remember.

'An amnesty'll bring him,' Bat Quinn said, heaving himself off his stool to lead the exodus from the bar. 'Good night to you so, girl.'

She was better at pouring the stout than her father was, even though he'd been at it for longer. Her hands were steadier, not yet roughened. She had the delicacy of the young, she'd heard her mother say when the disappointment about John Michael had become known.

'Good night, Fina,' the men called out, one after another before they left, and when the last of them had gone she bolted the door and urged her father to go upstairs to bed. She cleared up the glasses and knocked the contents of the ashtrays into a bowl. She wondered if they were sorry for her, Bat Quinn and the men John Michael had fished with, her mother and her father. Did they think of her as trapped among them, thrown there by the tide of circumstances, alone because she had misunderstood the nature of her love?

They could not know she had come to realize that she was less alone than if she were with John Michael now. The long companionship, their future planned, their passion and their embraces, were marked in memory with a poignancy from which the sting had been drawn. It was America they had loved, and loved too much. It was America that had enlivened love's fantasies, America that had enriched their delight in one another. He'd say that too if he came back when he'd made his money. They would walk again on the strand, neither of them mentioning the fragility of love, or the disaster that had been averted when they were young.

On the Streets

Arthurs ordered liver and peas and mashed potatoes in Strode Street. When it came, the liver didn't taste good. A skin of fat was beginning to congeal on the surface of the gravy where the potato hadn't soaked it up. The bright green peas were more or less all right.

He was a dark-haired man in his mid-fifties, with a widow's peak and lean features that matched his spare frame, bony wrists protruding from frayed white cuffs. He wore a black suit, its black trousers being a requirement for a breakfast waiter beneath a trim white jacket.

'You want a pot of tea with that?' the elderly woman who had brought him his plate of liver enquired. She came back to his table to ask him that, her only customer at this time in the afternoon.

Arthurs said yes. The woman wasn't a proper waitress; she didn't have a uniform, just a flowered overall folded over, tight on her stomach. Nearly seventy she'd be, he estimated, a woman who should be sitting by a fire somewhere, the heat bringing out crimson rings on her legs. He could sense her exhaustion, and wondered if she'd talk about it, if a conversation might develop.

'Finishing soon?' he said when she brought the tea,

speaking as if he knew her well, his tone suggesting that there'd been a past in their relationship, which there had not.

'I go at three-thirty.'

'Stop in tonight, will you?'

'Eh?' She looked at Arthurs with something like alarm in her tired eyes. Her hair was dyed yellowish, dewlaps of fat rolled over her neck. Widowed, he imagined.

'Reckon I'll stop in myself,' he said. 'Best if you're feeling dull.'

The woman answered none of that. He wondered if he should follow her when she finished for the day. It was twenty past three now and he'd be ready to go himself by half past. He broke the Garibaldi biscuit she'd brought with the tea. Since childhood he had followed people on the streets, to find out where they lived, to make a note of the address and add a few details that would remind him of the person. The compulsion was still insistent sometimes, but he could tell it wasn't going to be today.

'There's the television of course,' he said, 'if you're feeling not up to much.'

'No more'n rubbish these times,' the woman said, allowing herself that single comment only.

'Sends you to an early bed, does it?'

Again anxiety invaded the woman's eyes. She passed the tip of her tongue over her lips and wiped away the coating of saliva it left. Silent, she stumped off.

A pound and a few pence the bill came to when she brought it, food cheaper here when the busy lunchtime hours had passed. He'd known it would be cheaper, Arthurs reminded himself.

★

Mr Warkely came in and said don't start another batch or there'll be a clog-up in the dispatch room. So Cheryl turned the machine off and saw Mr Warkely glancing at the clock and noting the time on his pad. Finishing a quarter of an hour early would naturally have to be taken into account at the end of the week.

The Warkelys' business was in a small way, established three years ago in a basement, the retailing of scenic cards. Cheryl's task was to work the machine that encased in strong plastic wrapping each selection of six, together with the one that displayed in miniature the scenes each pack contained. It was part-time work, two hours three days a week; there was also, mornings only, the Costcutter checkout, office cleaning evenings.

The Warkelys employed no one else: Mrs Warkely attended to the accounts, the addressing of labels, and all correspondence; Mr Warkely packed the packaged selections into cardboard boxes and drove a van with *WPW Greetings Cards* on it. What was called the dispatch room was where television was watched, with the Warkelys' evening meal on two trays, evidence of their business stacked around the walls.

'See you Thursday,' Cheryl said before she went, and Mrs Warkely called out from somewhere and Mr Warkely grunted because his ballpoint was in his mouth. 'Thanks,' Cheryl said, which was what she always said when she left the basement. She didn't know why she did, but somehow that expression of gratitude seemed to round off the couple of hours better than just saying goodbye.

She banged the door behind her and climbed the steps to the street, a thin, smallish woman, grey in her hair now, lines gathering around her eyes and lips. She had been pretty once and still retained more than a vestige of those looks at fifty-one. Shabby in a maroon coat that once she'd been delighted to own and now disliked, her high-heeled shoes uncomfortable, she hurried on the street. There was no reason to hurry. She knew there was not and yet she hurried, her way of walking it had become.

'You getting on all right?' The voice came from behind her, the question asked by the man she'd once been married to, whom she'd thought of since as the error in her life. Always the same question it was when he was suddenly there on the street. She turned around.

'D'you want something?' She spoke sharply and he walked away at once, her tone causing offence. She knew it was that because it had happened often before. She had never told him what her hours at the Warkelys' were but he knew. He knew where her cleaning work was, he knew which Costcutter it was. Five months

the marriage had lasted, before she packed her belongings and went, giving up a full-time position in a Woolworth's, because she'd thought it better to move into
another district.

She stood where he had left her, watching him in
the distance until he turned a corner. 'I don't think you
should have married me,' she'd said, more or less what
Daph, who shared her counter in Woolworth's, had
been remorselessly repeating ever since the marriage
had taken place, not that she'd admitted to Daph that
things weren't right, not wanting to.

On the pavement she realized she was in the way of
two elderly women who were trying to pass. 'I'm
sorry,' she apologized and the women said it didn't
matter.

She walked on, more slowly than she'd been walking
before. When they married she had moved upstairs to
his two rooms, use of kitchen and bath, the rooms
freshly painted by him in honour of the change in both
their lives, old linoleum replaced by a carpet. The paint
had still been fresh when she left, the carpet unstained;
she'd never begun to call herself Mrs Arthurs.

*

Later that afternoon, although he was not a drinking
man, Arthurs entered a public house. Like the café in
which he had earlier had a meal, it was not familiar to
him: he liked new places.

He took the beer he ordered to a corner of the almost empty saloon bar, where the fruit machines were at rest, the music speakers silent. There was a griminess about the place, a gloom that inadequate lighting did not dispel. At the bar, on barstools, two men morosely sat without communicating. A shirt-sleeved barman turned the pages of the *Star*.

The dullness Arthurs had mentioned in the café possessed him entirely now, an infection it almost felt like, gathering and clinging to him, an unhealthy tepidness about it. He sipped the beer he'd ordered, wondering why he had come in here, wondering why he wasted money. Time was when he'd have gone to a racetrack, the dogs at Wimbledon or White City. In the crowd, with his mind on something else, he could have shaken off the mood. Or he might have rid himself of it by getting into conversation with a tart. Not that a tart had ever been much good, any more than the elderly waitress would have been. He closed his eyes, squeezing back disappointment at being asked if he wanted something when all he was doing was being friendly. They might have sat down somewhere, on a seat in a park, the flowerbeds just beginning to be colourful, birds floating on the water. She knew how it had been; she knew he'd gone there at last, today. In their brief encounter, she had guessed.

People began to come into the saloon bar, another lone man, couples. Arthurs watched them, picking out the ones he immediately disliked. He wondered about phoning up Mastyn's and saying he wouldn't be in in the morning. A stomach upset, he'd say. But the hours would hang heavy, because he'd wake anyway at twenty past five, being programmed to it. And there'd be nothing to replace the walk to the Underground, and the Underground itself, and walking the last bit to the hotel; and nothing to replace the three and a half hours in the dining-room until at half past ten he could hang up his white jacket and unhook his black bow tie. Since the hours of his employment at Mastyn's had been reduced, his earnings solely as a breakfast waiter were not enough to live on, but he made up the shortage in other ways. Since childhood he had stolen.

There was a telephone across the bar from where he sat, half obscured by a curtain drawn back from the entrance to the Ladies. Noticing it, he was tempted again. But whoever answered at the Reception would grumble, would say leave it until the morning, see how he was then. The conversation would be unsatisfactory, any message he left for the dining-room probably forgotten, and blame attached to him when he didn't turn up even though he'd done what was required of him. None of that was worth it.

Why had she spoken to him like that? Why had her voice gone harsh, asking him if he wanted something? He had never asked her for money, not once, yet the way she'd spoken you'd think he'd been for ever dropping hints. Music began, turned down low but noisy anyway because that was what it was, more a noise than anything else. The last couple who'd come in were noisy too, laughter that could have been kept quieter, both wearing dark glasses although there hadn't been sunshine all day. What he'd wanted to say was maybe they could go to a café for a few minutes. No more than that, ten minutes of her time.

Arthurs stared into the beer he hadn't drunk, at the scummy froth becoming nothing. The sympathy she could call upon was a depth in her, surprising in a woman who wasn't clever. He had been aware of it the first day on the stairs, when they'd got into conversation because he happened to be passing by. 'You like a cup of tea or something?' she'd offered, her key already in the lock of the door; and he'd said tea, two sugars, when they were in her room. He told her about the lunchtime complaint in the dining-room of Mastyn's because it was a natural thing to do; she said she'd wondered why he looked upset and then said anyone would be, a horrible thing to happen. He repeated the remarks that had been made, how he'd stood there having to listen, how the man had demanded the manager, how he'd said, 'We apologize for troubling you' when Mr Simoni came. Mr Simoni had held his hand out but they hadn't taken it.

Arthurs wondered for a moment if, that first day or later, he'd told her this too – that Mr Simoni's outstretched hand had been ignored. He couldn't remember saying it. A dotted bow-tie the man had been wearing, white dots on red, a chalk-striped shirt. The pepper had been ground over her risotto with a mutter that sounded insolent, the woman said. The coffee had been cold. 'Well, there'll certainly be no charge for the coffee,' Mr Simoni's immediate response was. Something special, this lunch should have been, the man said, and the woman called the lunch a misery before she threw her napkin down. They'd gone away, not knowing what they left behind. 'Breakfasts only after this,' Mr Simoni murmured while bowing and scraping to the people who'd gone silent at the other tables. 'Take it or not.' Beneath the thrown-down napkin there was a shopping list on a letter that had been half written and then abandoned, the shopping items pencilled on the space remaining. *Dear Sirs, An electric fire I purchased from you is faulty* had a jagged line drawn through it; there was a date in the same handwriting, and an address embossed in blue at the top of the single sheet.

Arthurs reached into an inside pocket and took from it this same writing paper, now folded to a quarter of its size. Frayed at the edges, it was dog-eared and soiled, one of the folds beginning to give way, and he didn't open it out for fear of damaging it further: it was enough to hold it for a moment between thumb and forefinger, to know that it was what he knew it was, kept by him always. A year ago he'd gone into a Kall-Kwik and had had it photographed twice, nervous in case one day the original might, somehow, not be there: he did not trust, and never had, any time that was yet to come or what might happen in it. He knew the address by heart, even in his sleep, in dreams; but who could tell what might happen to memory? Not that it mattered now, of course.

He returned the folded paper to his pocket and stood up. Seven o'clock she finished in the offices, ten past she was out on the streets again. Five to six it was and he sat for a little longer, thinking about her. For a long time before the day she'd asked him into her room he'd seen her coming and going. They had passed often on the stairs of the house where his own two rooms were a flight above hers, cheaper than the other rooms because of their bad state of repair. He hadn't known she was a widow, thinking her to be unmarried ever since she'd come to the house a year or so ago. A ticket man on the Underground apparently her husband had been.

He left his beer, pushing the glass away in case a sleeve caught it while he was putting his overcoat on. He buttoned the coat slowly – black like his suit – then crossed the saloon bar and stepped out into the darkening twilight. The folded paper was not something to keep, not any more, but even so he knew he could not destroy it. There was that, too, to tell her: that the shopping list would always be a memento.

★

Her encounter with her ex-husband had not particularly upset Cheryl: she was too used to his sudden appearances for that. As she emptied waste-paper baskets and gathered up plastic cups, uncoiled the long flex of her vacuum cleaner and began on the floors, she yet again blamed herself. She had been foolish. Lonely, she supposed, missing what death had taken from her, she had seen the man differently; it had felt natural, saying yes. Daph had been a witness in the register office, with a man they'd fetched in from the street. Afterwards they'd sat with Daph in the back bar of the Queen's Regiment and when a few people from the house turned up later they'd gone in a crowd to Bruce's Platter, above the Prudential Office. They'd kept calling her Mrs Arthurs, making a joke of it once the wine got going, but all that time he was very quiet until she heard him telling Daph about the lunchtime complaint, and every few minutes Daph – outspoken when she'd had a few too many – saying people like that didn't deserve a life. 'You hear that?' he said afterwards. 'What your friend remarked?'

At the time it had seemed ordinary enough that he should mention the complaint to someone else, that that terrible lunchtime should nag so, the wound of humiliation slow to heal. She had urged him to leave Mastyn's Hotel, to find another post in a restaurant or another hotel, but for whatever reason he wouldn't, stoically maintaining that being a lowly breakfast waiter was what he would remain now. She didn't understand that, although she accepted that when you married someone you took on his baggage, and one day the healing would be complete.

But on the night of her second marriage the baggage she'd taken on was suddenly more complicated. When they returned from the celebrations in the Queen's Regiment and Bruce's Platter her husband of half a day didn't want to go to bed. He said it was hardly worth it, since he had to get up soon after five. But it was not yet eleven when he said that.

Still vacuuming the office floors, Cheryl remembered the unflurried timbre of his voice when he offered this explanation, a matter-of-factness that, quite suddenly, made her feel cold. She remembered turning on the single bar of the electric fire she had brought upstairs from the room she no longer occupied. She remembered lying awake, wondering if the darkness of the bedroom would draw him to her, wondering if he was a man like that, not that she had ever heard of being like that before. But nothing happened except what was happening in her mind, the realization that she had made a mistake.

As she slid her vacuum cleaner into corners and under desks, all that was there again, as often it was when, on the streets, her ex-husband once more attempted to enter her life. A man who was hurt was what he'd seemed to be during the time they had been getting to know one another. She'd told him about times in her childhood, about her marriage, and the shock of widowhood; he'd spoken of the censure he'd always felt himself subjected to, culminating in the lunchtime complaint he'd taken so hard. Small rebukes, reproof, blame in its different forms affected him – she was sure – more than ever was intended: from the first she had known that, when each new shade of his accumulated pain was revealed to her. Then, too, she had believed that the pain would ease, as it seemed to when she was with him. But even before she packed her things to go, Daph said, 'Your guy's doolally.'

Cheryl turned the cleaner off and wound the flex back into place. She straightened the chairs she had had to move out of the way, finishing one office at a time and closing the door of each behind her. She took her coat and scarf from the hooks in the passage and carried downstairs the black plastic bag in which she'd collected the waste-paper. She re-set the night alarm. She banged the door behind her and began to walk away.

'They ignored Mr Simoni,' he said in the empty dark. 'Mr Simoni tried to shake hands with them but he needn't have bothered.'

★

She looked at him with nothing in her eyes. There was no flicker that they were man and wife, as if she had forgotten. She had been everything to him; she could have sensed it from the way he'd been with her. When they'd gone for a walk together, the second time they had, she'd put a hand on his arm. A Sunday that had been, a cold afternoon and she'd been wearing gloves, red and blue. Just a touch of pressure from her fingers, no more than that, nothing forward, but he'd felt the understanding there was. A waiter could tell you how people were, he had explained to her another time. She hadn't known it; she hadn't known how you could feel insulted, the amount people left beside a plate. Not that a breakfast waiter got anything at all.

'I don't want to stand here listening to you,' she said, and then she said he should see someone; she said she had asked him to leave her alone.

'It's just I wondered if I'd ever told you that, how Mr Simoni held out his hand.'

'Please leave me alone,' she said, walking on.

★

Every plea she made was a repetition, already stale before she made it, and sounding weary when she did. She had lost touch with Daph when she'd moved to another district but Daph had made her promise to go to the police if she became frightened.

'You could tell she was the kind of woman who complained,' he said. He'd put the coffee ready for her to pour out, but when he walked away she called after him that it was cold. You didn't expect there'd be a waiter with soiled cuffs in this dining-room, she said when Mr Simoni came.

Cheryl tried not to see when he rooted in a pocket for his wallet. It was worst of all, the grubby paper taken from his wallet and carefully unfolded, its tattered edges and the blue letters of the address offered to her as a gift might be. *Dear Sirs, I believe an electric fire I purchased* . . . In the dark she couldn't see but she knew the words were there, as the shopping list had been there too, before its pencilled items had all but disappeared.

'Please leave me alone,' she said.

Walking with her, he said the café by the launderette was always open, people waiting there for their washing to be ready. 'Quiet,' he said. 'Never less than quiet, that café.'

She could tell from his movements beside her that the paper was being folded again and then returned to the right compartment of his wallet. His wallet was small, black, its plastic coating worn away in places.

'It's hardly out of your way,' he said.

They were alone on the street; they had been since she'd heard his voice behind her saying that the people who'd complained had ignored Mr Simoni's wish to shake hands with them. He always spoke first from behind her on a street, his footsteps silent.

'I thought I might run into you today,' he said. 'She'll want to know about this morning, I thought.'

He mentioned tea and she said she didn't want tea at this hour. And then she thought that in a café she could raise her voice, drawing attention to his harassing of her. But she didn't want to go to a café with him.

When she'd found things he'd stolen he'd said nothing, not even shaking his head. When she'd packed her belongings he'd been silent too, as if expecting nothing better, humiliation self-inflicted now.

'Straight after I'd done at the hotel I went out there,' he said. 'This morning.'

He told her about the hotel people who'd had breakfast, a slack morning, being a Monday. He remembered the orders; he always could afterwards, even on a busy day, a waiter's skill, he called it. He told her about the bus he'd taken, out through Shepherd's Bush and Hammersmith and then the green of trees and grass beginning when Castelnau was left behind. Someone called out for the Red Rover and the driver shouted back that the Red Rover had gone years ago. There was a traffic hold-up at Upper Richmond Road and he got off and walked a bit. He'd been out there before, he said: Priory Lane, then left by a letter-box. A dozen times, he said, he'd checked it out.

They turned a corner and she could see the lit-up window of the launderette. She remembered the café he was talking about then, a little further along with a 7-Up sign in the window.

'I've something to get washed,' he said.

She didn't go into the launderette with him. While he was there she could have hurried on, past the café, to where the buses ran. Any bus would have done, even one going in the wrong direction. But in the café, where an elderly man and two women on their own were the only customers, she carried from the counter a pot of tea and two glass cups and saucers, and went back for milk.

She waited then, blankly staring at the tea she'd poured, taking the first sip, tasting nothing. No thoughts disturbed her. She did not feel she was in a café, only that she was alone, anywhere it could have been; and then her thoughts began again. She had been drawn to him; that reminder echoed, hardly anything else made sense.

She watched him coming in, the door slipping closed behind him. He looked about, knowing she would be there, knowing she wouldn't have disappeared.

★

On the table he laid out what he had taken from the pockets of his jacket before he'd put it into a washing machine: keys, his wallet, a ballpoint. He had thought she would ask about his jacket, where it was, why he wasn't wearing it, but she didn't. He stirred the tea she'd poured for him. It didn't matter that she didn't ask; his overcoat was open, she could see the jacket wasn't there.

'Three hours ago he'll have found her,' he said. 'A quarter past seven every evening he gets back to that house.'

★

Cheryl stared at a cigarette burn on the table's surface while he told her. He had rung the bell, he said, and the woman hadn't recognized him when she opened the door. He'd said he'd come to read the meter, not saying which one. The gas man had been, no longer than a week ago, the woman had said, and he'd apologized for not having his badge on display. He'd pulled aside his overcoat to show the electricity badge on his left lapel. The woman hadn't closed the door when he walked into the hall. A good ten minutes it was open before his hands were free to close it.

'I blame myself,' he said, 'for being stupid like that.' He added that he didn't blame himself for anything else; he had stood there, not blaming himself, remembering the woman saying that his cuffs were grimy, complaining that the coffee was cold. He had stood there, hearing her voice, and the telephone rang on a small table near the hallstand. When it stopped he went to wash his hands in the downstairs lavatory, where coats and the man's hats and a cap hung on hooks. In the hall he draped a tissue over the Yale latch before he turned it; and afterwards dropped the scrunched-up tissue into a waste-bin on a lamp post.

Cheryl didn't say anything; she never did. She watched while his overcoat was buttoned again after she'd seen he wasn't wearing his jacket. A dribble of blood from the woman's mouth had got on to his sleeve, he said, the kind of thing that was discernible beneath a microscope, easy to overlook.

Once he'd shown her a bruise he'd acquired on a finger while he was committing his crime, another time he'd shown her the tissue he had draped over the Yale, forgotten in his pocket all day. Once he'd said the second post had come while he was there, brown envelopes mostly, clattering through the letter-box. While the woman was on the floor there'd been the postman's whistling and his footsteps going away.

'I didn't take a bus,' he said. 'I didn't want that, sitting on a bus. The first food I had afterwards was liver and peas.'

The last time it had been a packet of crisps; another time, a chicken burger. Still silent, Cheryl listened while his voice continued, while he explained that ever since this morning he'd felt she was his only friend, ever since he'd washed his hands, with the man's coats on coat-hangers and the scented soap on its own special little porcelain shelf. A cat had jumped on to the windowsill outside and begun to mew, as if it knew what had occurred. He had thought of opening the back door to let it in, so that it would be in the hall when the man returned, and its bloody footsteps all over the house.

She had never told Daph that it wasn't fear she experienced when she was with him, that it wasn't even disquiet. She had never said she knew there was cunning in his parade of what hadn't happened, yet that it hardly seemed like cunning, so little did he ask of her. She had never said she knew it was her nature that had drawn her to go for walks with him and to accept his reticent embrace, that her pity was his nourishment. She had never wanted to talk to Daph about him. The Warkelys didn't know he existed.

He lifted the glass cup to his lips. She still did not speak. It was not necessary to speak, only to remain a little longer, the silence an element in being with him. He did not follow her when she walked away.

He would finish his tea and pour another cup: on the streets again she imagined that. In the launderette he would open the door of a machine and release his sodden jacket from where it clung to the drum. He would spread out the sleeves and pull the material back into shape before he began his journey to the rooms where so briefly they had lived together. He would not, tonight, be offended by the glare of neon beneath which she now walked herself. Nor by the cars that loitered in their search for what the night had to offer. Nor by the voices of the couples pressed close to one another as they went by. Her tears, tonight, allowed him peace.

The Dancing-Master's Music

Brigid's province was the sculleries, which was where
you began if you were a girl, the cutlery room and the
boot room if you weren't. Brigid began when she was
fourteen and she was still fourteen when she heard
about the dancing-master. It was Mr Crome who talked
about him first, whose slow, lugubrious delivery came
through the open scullery door from the kitchen. Lily
Geoghegan said Mr Crome gave you a sermon whenever he opened his mouth.

'An Italian person, we are to surmise. From the
Italian city of Naples. A travelling person.'

'Well, I never,' Mrs O'Brien interjected, and Brigid
could tell she was busy with something else.

The sculleries were low-ceilinged, with saucepans
and kettles hanging on pot-hooks, and the bowls and
dishes and jelly-moulds which weren't often in use
crowding the long shelf that continued from one scullery to the next, even though there was a doorway
between the two. Years ago the door that belonged in
it had been taken off its hinges because it was in the
way, but the hinges were left behind, too stiff to move
now. Flanked with wide draining-boards, four slate
sinks stretched beneath windows that had bars on the

outside, and when the panes weren't misted Brigid could see the yard sheds and the pump. Once in a while one of the garden boys drenched the cobbles with buckets of water and swept them clean.

'Oh, yes,' Mr Crome went on. 'Oh, yes, indeed. That city famed in fable.'

'Is it Italian steps he's teaching them, Mr Crome?'

'Austria is the source of the steps, we have to surmise. I hear Vienna mentioned. Another city of renown.'

Mr Crome's sermon began then, the history of the waltz step, and Brigid didn't listen. From the sound of the range dampers being adjusted, the oven door opened and closed, she could tell that Mrs O'Brien wasn't listening either.

Nobody listened much to Mr Crome when he got going, when he wasn't cross, when he wasn't giving out about dust between the banister supports or the fires not right or a staleness on the water of the carafes. You listened then all right, no matter who you were.

Every morning, early, Brigid walked from Glenmore, over Skenakilla Hill to Skenakilla House. She waited at the back door until John or Thomas opened it. If Mr Crome kept her on, if she gave satisfaction and was conscientious, if her disposition in the sculleries turned out to be agreeable, she would lodge in. Mr Crome had explained that, using those words and expressions. She was glad she didn't have to live in the house immediately.

Brigid was tall for her age, surprising Mr Crome

when she told him what it was. Fair-haired and freckled, she was the oldest of five, a country girl from across the hill. 'Nothing much in the way of looks,' Mr Crome confided in the kitchen after he'd interviewed her. Her mother he remembered well, for she had once worked in the sculleries herself, but unfortunately had married Ranahan instead of advancing in her employment, and was now – so Mr Crome passed on to Mrs O'Brien – brought low by poverty and childbirth. Ranahan was never sober.

Brigid was shy in the sculleries at first. The others glanced in when they passed, or came to look at her if they weren't pressed. When they spoke to her she could feel a warmth coming into her face and the more she was aware of it the more it came, confusing her, sometimes making her say what she didn't intend to say. But when a few weeks had gone by all that was easier, and by the time the dancing-master arrived in the house she didn't find even dinnertime the ordeal it had been at first.

'Where's Naples, Mr Crome?' Thomas asked in the servants' dining-room on the day Mr Crome first talked about Italy. 'Where'd it be placed on the map, Mr Crome?'

He was trying to catch Mr Crome out. Brigid could see Annie-Kate looking away in case she giggled, and Lily Geoghegan's elbow nudged by the tip of John's. Nodding and smiling between her mouthfuls, deaf to all that was said, but with flickers of ancient beauty still alive in her features, Old Mary sat at the other end of the long table at which Mr Crome presided. Beside him, Mrs O'Brien saw that he was never without mashed potato on his plate, specially mashed, for Mr Crome would not eat potatoes served otherwise. The Widow Kinawe, who came on Mondays and Thursdays for the washing and was sometimes on the back avenue when Brigid reached it in the mornings, sat next to her at the table, with Jerety from the garden on the other side, and the garden boys beside him.

'Naples is washed by the sea,' Mr Crome said.

'I'd say I heard a river mentioned, Mr Crome. It wouldn't be a river it's washed by?'

'What you heard, boy, was the River Danube. Nowhere near.' And Mr Crome traced the course of that great river, taking a chance here and there in his version of its itinerary. It was a river that gave its name to a waltz, which would be why Thomas heard it mentioned.

'Well, that beats Banagher!' Mrs O'Brien said.

Mrs O'Brien often said that. In the dining-room next to the kitchen the talk was usually of happenings in the house, of arrivals and departures, news received, announcements made, anticipations: Mrs O'Brien's expression of wonderment was regularly called upon. John and Thomas, or the two bedroom maids, or Mr Crome himself, brought from the upper rooms the harrowings left behind after drawing-room conversation or dining-room exchanges, or chatter anywhere at all. 'Harrowings' was Mrs O'Brien's word, servitude's share of the household's chatter.

It was winter when Brigid began in the sculleries and when the dancing-master came to the house. Every evening she would return home across the hill in the dark, but after the first few times she knew the way well, keeping to the stony track, grateful when there was moonlight. She took with her, once in four weeks, the small wage Mr Crome paid her, not expecting more until she was trained in the work. When it rained she managed as best she could, drying her clothes in the hearth when she got home, the fire kept up for that purpose. When it rained in the mornings she could feel the dampness pressed on her all day.

The servants were what Brigid knew of Skenakilla House. She heard about the Master and Mrs Everard and the family, about Miss Turpin and Miss Roche, and the grandeur of the furniture and the rooms. She imagined them, but she had not ever seen them. The reality of the servants when they sat down together at dinnertime she brought home across Skenakilla Hill: long-faced Thomas, stout John, Old Mary starting conversations that nobody kept going, Lily Geoghegan and Annie-Kate giggling into their food, the lugubriousness of Mr Crome, Mrs O'Brien flushed and flurried when she was busy. She told of the disappointments that marked the widowhood of the Widow Kinawe, of Jerety wordless at the dinner table, his garden boys silent also.

'Ah, he's no size at all. Thin as a knife-blade,' was the hearsay that Brigid took across Skenakilla Hill when the dancing-master arrived. 'Black hair, like Italians have. A shine to it.'

At one and the same time he played the piano and taught the steps, Mr Crome said, and recalled another dancing-master, a local man from the town, who had brought a woman to play the piano and a fiddler to go with her. Buckley that man was called, coming out to the house every morning in his own little cart, with his retinue.

'Though for all that,' Mr Crome said, 'I doubt he had the style of the Italian man. I doubt Buckley had the bearing.'

Once Brigid heard the music, a tinkling of the piano keys that lasted only as long as the green, baize-covered door at the end of the kitchen passage was open. John's shoulder held it wide while he passed through with a tray of cups and saucers. At the time, Annie-Kate was showing Brigid how to fill the oil lamps in the passage, which soon would become one of her duties if Mr Crome decided she was satisfactory. Until that morning she had never been in the passage before, the sculleries being on the other side of the kitchen wing. 'That same old tune,' Annie-Kate said. 'He never leaves it.' But Brigid would have listened for longer and was disappointed when the baize door closed and the sound went with it. It was the first time she had heard a piano played.

Three days later, at dinnertime, Mr Crome said:

'The Italian has done with them. On Friday he'll pack his traps and go on to Skibbereen.'

'Can they do the steps now, Mr Crome?' Annie-Kate asked, in the pert manner she sometimes put on at the dinner table when she forgot herself. Once Brigid heard Mrs O'Brien call it cheek, giving out to Annie-Kate in the kitchen, and Annie-Kate came into the sculleries afterwards, red-faced and tearful, dabbing at her face with her apron, not minding being seen by Brigid, the way she would by the others.

'That is not for us to know,' Mrs O'Brien reprimanded her, but Mr Crome pondered the question. It was a safe assumption, he suggested eventually, that the dancing-master wouldn't be leaving unless the purpose of his visit had been fulfilled. He interrupted a contribution on the subject from John to add:

'It's not for that I mention it. On Thursday night he is to play music to us.'

'What d'you mean, Mr Crome?' Mrs O'Brien was startled by the news, and Brigid remembered hearing Lily Geoghegan once whispering to Annie-Kate that Mrs O'Brien was put out when she wasn't told privately and in advance anything of importance in Mr Crome's news.

'I'll tell you what I mean, Mrs O'Brien. It's that every man jack of us will sit down upstairs, that John and Thomas will carry up to the drawing-room the chairs we are occupying this minute and arrange them as directed by myself, that music will be played for us.'

'Why's that, Mr Crome?' Annie-Kate asked.

'It's what has been arranged, Annie. It's what we're being treated to on Thursday evening.'

'We're never sitting down with the Master and Mrs Everard? With the girls and Miss Turpin and Miss Roche? You're having us on, Mr Crome!' Annie-Kate laughed and Lily Geoghegan laughed, and John and Thomas. Old Mary joined in.

But Mr Crome had never had anyone on in his life. For the purpose of the dancing-master's recital, the drawing-room would be vacated by the family, he explained. The family would have heard the music earlier that same day, in the late afternoon. It was a way of showing gratitude to the dancing-master for his endeavours that he was permitted to give his performance a second time.

'Is it the stuff he's always hammering out we'll have to listen to?' Annie-Kate asked. 'The waltz steps, is it, Mr Crome?'

Mr Crome shook his head. He had it personally from Miss Turpin that the music selected by the dancing-master was different entirely. It was music that was suitable for the skill he possessed at the piano, not composed by himself, yet he knew every note off by heart and didn't need to read off a page.

'Well, I never!' Mrs O'Brien marvelled, mollified because all that Mr Crome said by way of explanation had been directly addressed to her, irrespective of where the queries came from.

★

On that Thursday evening, although Brigid didn't see the Master or Mrs Everard, or the girls, or Miss Turpin or Miss Roche, she saw the drawing-room. At the end of a row, next to the Widow Kinawe, she took her place on one of the round-bottomed chairs that had been arranged at Mr Crome's instruction, and looked about her. A fire blazed at either end of the long, shadowy room and, hanging against scarlet wallpaper, there were gilt-framed portraits, five on one wall, four on another. There were lamps on the mantelpiece and on tables, a marble figure in a corner, the chairs and the sofa the family sat on all empty now. A grand piano had pride of place.

Brigid had never seen a portrait before. She had never seen such furniture, or two fires in a room. She had never seen a piano, grand or otherwise. On the wide boards of the floor, rugs were spread, and in a whisper the Widow Kinawe drew her attention to the ceiling, which was encrusted with a pattern of leaves and flowers, all in white.

Small, and thin as a knife-blade, just as she had described him herself, the dancing-master brought with him a scent of oil when he arrived, a lemony smell yet with a sweetness to it. He entered the drawing-room, closed the door behind him, and went quickly to the piano, not looking to either side of him. He didn't speak, but sat down at once, clasped his hands together, splayed his fingers, exercising them before he began. All the time he played the music, the scent of oil was there, subtle in the warm air of the drawing-room.

There had been a fiddler at the wake of Brigid's grandmother. He was an old man who suffered from the coldness, who sat close in to the hearth and played a familiar dirge and then another and another. There was keening and after it the tuneless sound continued, the fiddler hunched over the glow of the turf, Brigid's grandmother with her hands crossed on her funeral dress in the other room. But while the lamplight flickered and the two fires blazed, the dancing-master's music was different in every way from the fiddler's. It scurried and hurried, softened, was calm, was slow. It danced over the scarlet walls and the gaze of the portrait people. It lingered on the empty chairs, on vases and ornaments. It rose up to reach the white flowers of the encrusted ceiling. Brigid closed her eyes and the dancing-master's music crept about her darkness, its tunes slipping away, recalled, made different. There was the singing of a thrush. There was thunder far away, and the stream she went by on Skenakilla Hill, rushing, then babbling. The silence was different when the music stopped, as if the music had changed it.

The dancing-master stood up then and bowed to the

congregated servants, who bowed back to him, not knowing what else to do. He left the drawing-room, still without saying anything, and the round-bottomed chairs were carried back to where they'd come from. Brigid caught a glimpse of Lily Geoghegan and John kissing while she was getting herself ready for the walk across the hill. 'Well, there's skill in it all right,' was Mr Crome's verdict on the dancing-master's performance, but Thomas said he'd been looking forward to a few jigs and Annie-Kate complained that she'd nearly died, sitting on a hard chair for an hour and a half. The Widow Kinawe said it was great to see inside a room the like of that, twenty-three pieces of china she'd counted. Old Mary hadn't heard a thing, but still declared she'd never spent a better evening. 'Who was that man at all?' she asked Mrs O'Brien, whose eyes had closed once or twice, but not as Brigid's had.

That February night on the stony hillside track there was frost in the air and the sky was blazing with stars that seemed to Brigid to be a further celebration of the music she'd heard, of beauty and of a feeling in herself. The tunes she tried for eluded her, but somehow it was right that they should, that you couldn't just reach out for them. The hurrying and the slowness and the calm, the music made of the stream she walked by now, weren't perfect, as when she'd closed her eyes in the drawing-room. But crossing Skenakilla Hill, Brigid took with her enough of what there had been, and it was still enough when she woke in the morning, and still enough when she worked again in the sculleries.

Mr Crome said at dinnertime that the dancing-master had left the house after breakfast. One last time he'd gone through the waltz steps. Then he left for Skibbereen.

★

Only once in the weeks and months that followed did the Italian dancing-master come up in conversation. Mrs O'Brien wondered where his travels had taken him, which caused Mr Crome to draw on his conversations with Miss Turpin and Miss Roche. The dancing-master, true enough, was a wandering stone. The chances were that he was in England or perhaps in France; and Spain and India had been spoken of. One fact that could be stated with confidence, Mr Crome assured his fellow-servants: long ago the dancing-master would have shaken the dust of Skibbereen from his heels. 'And who'd blame him?' Thomas muttered, chewing hard on gristle until surreptitiously he took it from his mouth.

That was the last time in the dining-room next to the kitchen, or anywhere else where the servants conversed, that the visit of the dancing-master to Skenakilla House was talked about. The event passed into the shadows of their memory, the gathering in the drawing-room touched in the recall of some with tedium. Other instances more readily claimed attention: heatwaves and storms, winter nights that froze the pump in the yard, props made for two of the cherry trees.

But for Brigid the music kept faith with her and she with it. The dancing-master splayed his fingers while the two fires burned in the drawing-room and the eyes looked down from the walls. In the sculleries where no man loved her as John loved Lily Geoghegan, the music rose on a crescendo and settled to a whisper. She brought it to the bedroom that in time she came to share with Lily Geoghegan and Annie-Kate. She brought it to the garden where, every day, her task was to cut whatever herbs were wanted. On Sunday afternoons when she walked to Glenmore through the solitude of Skenakilla Hill, the stars that had lit a February sky were still a celebration.

Advancing in her employment, Brigid was permitted to know the house and the family, and always stopped whatever she was doing in another room when the sound of the piano reached her. She heard it with pleasure, but nothing in it haunted her or stayed with her afterwards, even vaguely or uncertainly. At first she hoped that the same piano would one day bring her the dancing-master's music, but she was glad in the end that the music was not played by someone else.

It belonged with the dancing-master on his travels, and Brigid imagined great houses in England and France, seeing them as clearly as looking at pictures in a book. Grey elephants ambled through the bright heat of India, pale palaces in Spain echoed with the dancing-master's skill. There was the church of the dancing-master's city, and the priests waiting with the Host.

A time came when there was no longer a reason for Brigid to walk to Glenmore on Sunday afternoons, there being no one left in Glenmore to visit. In that same year Mr Crome gave up his position to a new man who had come; not long after that one of the garden boys took over from Mr Jerety. Old Mary had gone long ago; one morning Mrs O'Brien was found dead.

A time came later when the fortunes of the family declined. The trees were felled for timber. Slates blown from the roof were left where they lay. In forgotten rooms cobwebs gathered; doors were closed on must and mildew. The servants' dining-room was abandoned because there weren't servants enough to sit round the table.

With great sadness, Brigid witnessed the spread of this deterioration, the house gone quiet in its distress, the family broken. But as if nothing had happened, as if no change had occurred, the dancing-master's music did not cease. It was there in the drawing-room where the vases were empty of flowers and the ceiling dark with smoke and the covers of the sofas marked by the sun. Untouched, unaffected, it cheered the sculleries and the kitchen and the yard. It danced over dust and decay in the hall and the passageways, on landings and stairs. It was there with the scents of the herb garden, tarragon and thyme half stifled.

No longer possessing the strength to stroll on Skenakilla Hill, Brigid looked out from the windows of the house to where tree stumps were the remnant of the hillside woods. As old now as she remembered Old Mary being, it was with difficulty that she discerned the stream and the track, but each time she looked from the windows she managed to do so in the end. She knew with the certainty of instinct that the dancing-master's music was there too. She knew it would be there when she was gone, the marvel in her life a ghost for the place.

A Bit on the Side

In the Japanese café he helped her off with her coat and took it to the line of hooks beneath the sign that absolved the management of responsibility for its safety. They weren't the first in the café, although it was early, ten past eight. The taxi-driver who came in most mornings was reading the *Daily Mail* in his usual corner. Two of the music students had arrived.

He hung up the coat, which still carried a faint trace of scent. Lightweight, and black, its showerproof finish was protection enough today, since the forecast they'd both heard – she in her kitchen an hour ago, he while he shaved in Dollis Hill – confidently predicted that the fine weather was here for another few days. He hadn't brought a coat himself and he didn't wear a hat in summer.

From the table they always sat at, side by side so that they could see the street where the office workers were beginning to hurry by, she watched him patting a pocket of his jacket, making sure his cigarettes and lighter were there. Something was different this morning; on the walk from Chiltern Street she had sensed, for an instant only, that their love affair was not as it had been yesterday. Almost always they met in Chiltern

Street, their two journeys converging there. Neither ever waited: when one or other was late they made do with meeting in the café.

'All right?' she asked. 'All right?' She kept anxiety out of her tone; no need for it, why should there be? She knew about the touchiness of love: almost always, it was misplaced.

'Absolutely,' he said, and then their coffee came, his single croissant with it, the Japanese waitress smiling. 'Absolutely,' he repeated, breaking his croissant in half.

Another of the music students arrived, the one with the clarinet case. Then a couple from the hotel in George Street came in, Americans, who sat beneath the picture of the sea wave, whose voices – ordering scrambled eggs and ham – placed them geographically. The regular presence of such visitors from overseas suggested that breakfast in the nearby hotel was more expensive than it was here.

The lovers who had met in Chiltern Street were uneasy, in spite of efforts made by both of them. Discomfiture had flickered in his features when he'd been asked if everything was all right: now, at least, that didn't show. She hadn't been convinced by his reassurance and, within minutes, her own attempt to reassure herself hadn't made much sense: this, in turn, she kept hidden.

She reached out to flick a flake of croissant from his chin. It was the kind of thing they did, he turning up the collar of her coat when it was wrong, she straightening his tie. Small gestures made, their way of possessing one another in the moments they made their own, not that they ever said.

'I just thought,' she began to say, and watched him shake his head.

'How good you look!' he murmured softly. He stroked the back of her hand with his fingertips, which he often did, just once, the same brief gesture.

'I miss you all the time,' she said.

She was thirty-nine, he in his mid-forties. Their relationship had begun as an office romance, before computers and their software filched a living from her. She had moved on of necessity, he of necessity had remained: he had a family to support in Dollis Hill. These days they met as they had this morning, again at lunchtime in the Paddington Street Gardens or the picture gallery where surreptitiously they ate their sandwiches when it was wet, again at twenty to six in the Running Footman.

He was a man who should have been, in how he dressed, untidy. His easy, lazily expansive gestures, his rugged, often sunburnt features, his fair hair stubborn in its disregard of his intentions, the weight he was inclined to put on, all suggested a nature that would resist sartorial demands. In fact, he was quite dressily turned out, this morning in pale lightweight trousers and jacket, blue Eton shirt, his tie striped blue and red. It was a contradiction in him she had always found attractive.

She herself, today, besides the black of her showerproof coat, wore blue and green, the colours repeated in the flimsy silk of her scarf. Her smooth black hair was touched with grey which she made no attempt to disguise, preferring to make the most of what the approach of middle age allowed. She would have been horrified if she'd put on as much as an ounce; her stratagems saw to it that she didn't. Eyes, nose, mouth, cheeks, unblemished neck: no single feature stood out, their combination necessary in the spare simplicity of her beauty. Good earrings – no more than dots, and never absent – were an emphasis that completed what was already there.

'Have your cigarette,' she said.

He slipped the cellophane from a packet of Marlboro. They talked about the day, predicting what it would bring. She was secretary to a businessman, the managing director of a firm that imported fashion clothes, he an accountant. A consignment of Italian trouser-suits had failed to reach the depot in Shoreditch, had still been missing the evening before. She spoke of that; he of a man called Bannister, in the patio business, who had been under-declaring his profits, which meant he would have to be dismissed as a client. He had been written to yesterday: this morning there'd be an outraged telephone call in response.

The taxi-driver left the café, since it was almost half past eight now and the first of the traffic wardens would be coming on. From where they sat they watched him unlock his cab, parked across the street. With its orange light gleaming, he drove away.

'You're worried,' she said, not wanting to say it, pursuing what she sensed was best left.

He shook his head. Bannister had been his client, his particularly, he said; he should have known. But it wasn't that and she knew it wasn't. They were lying to one another, she suddenly thought, lies of silence or whatever the term was. She sensed their lies although she hardly knew what her own were, in a way no more than trying to hide her nervousness.

'They suit you,' he said. 'Your Spanish shoes.'

They'd bought them, together, two days ago. She'd asked and the girl had said they were Spanish. He'd noticed them this morning in Chiltern Street, the first time she'd worn them. He'd meant to say they suited her then, but the bagwoman who was usually in Chiltern Street at that time had shuffled by and he'd had to grope in his pocket for her twenty pence.

'They're comfortable,' she said. 'Surprisingly so.'

'You thought they mightn't be.'

'Yes, I did.'

It was here, at this same table, that she had broken the news of her divorce, not doing so – not even intimating her intentions – until her marriage's undoing was absolute. Her quiet divorce, she had called it, and didn't repeat her husband's protest when the only reason she had offered him was that their marriage had fallen apart. 'No, there is no one else,' she had deftly prevaricated, and hadn't passed that on either. 'I would have done it anyway,' she had insisted in the café, though knowing that she might not have. She was happier, she had insisted too. She felt uncluttered, a burden of duty and restriction lifted from her. She'd wanted that.

'Wire gauze, I suppose,' he said, the subject now a cat that was a nuisance, coming in the bedroom windows of his house.

Although such domestic details were sometimes touched upon – his house, his garden, the neighbour-hood of Dollis Hill – his family remained mysterious, never described or spoken of. Since the divorce, he had visited the flat her husband had moved out of, completing small tasks for her, a way of being involved in another part of her life. But her flat never seemed quite right, so used had they become to their love affair conducted elsewhere and differently.

He paid and left a tip. He picked up his old, scuffed briefcase from where he'd leant it against a leg of their table, then held her coat for her. Outside, the sun was just becoming warm. She took his arm as they turned from Marylebone High Street into George Street. These streets and others like them were where their love affair belonged, its places – more intimately – the Japanese café and the Paddington Street Gardens, the picture gallery, the Running Footman. This part of London felt like home to both of them, although her flat was miles away, and Dollis Hill further still.

They walked on now, past the grey bulk of the Catholic church, into Manchester Square, Fitzhardinge Street, then to her bus stop. Lightly they embraced when the bus came. She waved when she was safely on it.

★

Walking back the way they'd come, he didn't hurry, his battered briefcase light in his right hand, containing only his lunchtime sandwiches. He passed the picture gallery again, scaffolding ugly on its façade. A porter was polishing the brass of the hotel doors, people were leaving the church.

Still slowly, he made his way to Dorset Street, where his office was. When she'd worked there, too, everyone had suspected and then known – but not that sometimes in the early morning, far earlier than this, they had crept together up the narrow stairs, through a dampish smell before the air began to circulate in the warren that partitions created. The wastepaper baskets had usually been cleared the night before, perfunctory hoovering had taken place; a tragedy it always was if the cleaners had decided to come in the morning instead and still were there.

All that seemed long ago now and yet a vividness remained: the cramped space on the floor, the hurrying, footsteps heard suddenly on the stairs, dust brushed from her clothes before he attended to his own. Even when she was no longer employed there they had a couple of times made use of the office in the early morning, but she had never wanted to and they didn't any more. Too far away to be visited at lunchtime, her flat had never come into its own in this way after the divorce. Now and again, not often, he managed a night there, and it was then that there were the tasks she had saved up for him, completed before they left together in the morning.

He thought about her, still on her bus, downstairs near the back, her slim black handbag on her lap, her Spanish shoes. What had she noticed? Why had she said, 'All right?' and said it twice? Not wanting to, and trying not to, he had passed on a mood that had begun in him, the gnawing of a disquiet he didn't want to explain because he wasn't able to, because he didn't understand it. When she'd said she missed him all the time, he should have said he missed her in that same way, because he did, because he always had.

When he had settled himself in the partitioned area of office space allocated to him, when he had opened the window and arranged in different piles the papers that constituted the work he planned for the morning, the telephone rang.

'Hey!' the voice of the patio-layer, Bannister, rumbustiously protested. 'What's all this bloody hoo-ha then?'

★

'It would have been Tuesday,' she said. 'Tuesday of last week. The twenty-fourth.'

There was silence, a muffled disturbance then, a hand placed over the receiver.

'We'll ring you back,' someone she hadn't been talking to before promised. 'Five minutes.'

The consignment of trouser suits had gone to York, another voice informed her when she telephoned again. There was ninety per cent certainty about that. The Salvadore dresses had been on their way to York; the trouser suits must somehow have taken that route too.

Hours later, when the morning had passed, when there'd been further telephone calls and faxes sent and faxes received, when the missing trouser-suits had definitely been located in York, when they'd been loaded on to a van and conveyed at speed to London, the crisis was recounted in the Paddington Street Gardens. So was the fury of the patio-layer Bannister, the threats of legal action, the demands that fees already charged and paid should in the circumstances be returned.

'Could he have a case?' Not just politely, she took an interest, imagining the anger on the telephone, the curt responses to it, for naturally no sympathy could be shown.

Listening, she opened the plastic container of the salad she had picked up on her way from the Prêt à Manger in Orchard Street. He had already unwrapped his sandwiches, releasing a faint whiff of Marmite.

Edges of lettuce poked out from between slices of white bread. Not much nourishment in that, she'd thought when first she'd seen his sandwiches, but had not said. There usually was egg or tomato as well, which was better; made for him that morning in Dollis Hill.

Small and sedate – no walking on the grass – the Gardens were where a graveyard once had been, which for those who knew added a frisson to the atmosphere. But bright with roses today, there was nothing sombre about the place for those who didn't. Girls sunbathed in this brief respite from being inside, men without their jackets strolled leisurely about. A lawnmower was started up by a young man with a baseball cap turned back to front. Escaping from a Walkman, jazz for an instant broke the Gardens' rule and was extinguished swiftly.

She didn't want the salad she was eating. She wanted to replace the transparent lid and carry the whole thing to one of the black rubbish bins, and then sit down again beside him and take his hand, not saying anything. She wanted them to sit there while he told her what the trouble was, while all the other office people went away and the Gardens were empty except for them- selves and the young mothers with their children in the distant playground. She wanted to go on sitting there, not caring, either of them, about the afternoon that did not belong to them. But she ate slowly on, as he did too, pigeons hovering a yard away.

It was the divorce, she speculated; it was the faltering at last of his acceptance of what she'd done. It wasn't difficult to imagine him lying awake at nights, more and more as time went by, for longer and longer, feeling trapped by the divorce. He would hear the breathing of his wife, a murmur from a dream; a hand would involuntarily reach out. He would watch light breaking the dark, slivers at first at the edges of the curtains through which marauding cats had been known to pass. He would try to think of something else, to force into his consciousness a different time of his life, childhood, the first day in an office and all the strangeness there had been. But always, instead, there was what there was.

'It's over, isn't it?' she said.

He screwed up the foil that had wrapped his sand-wiches and lobbed it into the bin nearest to where they sat. He nearly always didn't miss. He didn't now.

'I'm using up your life,' he said.

Her unfinished salad was on the seat between them, where his briefcase was too. When they'd been em-ployed in the same office their surreptitious lunches among the dozy attendants in the picture gallery hadn't been necessary when it rained; there'd been the privacy of his partitioned space, a quietness in the building then, sometimes a transistor playing gently behind a closed door, usually not even that. But always they had preferred their picnic in the Gardens.

'It's what I want,' she said.

'You deserve much more.'

'Is it the divorce?' And in the same flat tone she added, 'But I wanted that too, you know. For my own sake.'

He shook his head. 'No, not the divorce,' he said.

★

'No end to the heatwave they can't see,' Nell the tea-woman remarked, pouring his tea from a huge metal teapot, milk already added, two lumps of sugar on the saucer. She was small and wiry, near the end of her time: when she went there'd be a drinks machine instead.

'Thanks, Nell,' he said.

It wasn't the divorce. He had weathered the tremors of the divorce, had admired – after the shock of hearing what so undramatically she had done – her calm resolve. He had let her brush away his nervousness, his alarm at first that this was a complication that, emotionally, might prove too much for both of them.

Sipping his milky tea, he experienced a pang of desire, sharp as a splinter, an assault on his senses and his heart that made him want to go to her now, to clatter down the uncarpeted stairs and out into the fresh summer air, to take a taxi-cab, a thing he never did, to ask for her in the much smarter office building that was hers, and say when she stepped out of the lift that of course they could not do without one another.

He shuffled through the papers that were his afternoon's work. *I note your comments regarding Section TMA (1970),* he read, *but whilst it is Revenue policy not to invoke the provisions of Section 88 unless there is substantial delay it is held that when the delay continues beyond the following April 5 these provisions are appropriate. Under all the circumstances, I propose to issue an estimated assessment which will make good an apparent loss of tax due to the Crown.*

He scribbled out his protest and added it to the pile for typing. She was the stronger of the two, stoical, and being stoical was what he'd always loved. Deprived of what they had, she would manage better, even if the circumstances suggested that she wouldn't.

★

He wasn't in the Running Footman when she arrived. He usually was, and no matter what, she knew he'd come. When he did, he bought their drinks, since this evening it was his turn. He carried them to where she had kept a seat for him. Sherry it was for her, medium dry. His was the week's red wine, from Poland. Muzak was playing, jazzy and sentimental.

'I'm sorry,' he said before he said anything else.

'I'm happy, you know.' She intended to say more. She'd thought all that out during the afternoon, her sentences composed and ready. But in his company she was aware that none of that was necessary: it was he, not she, who had to do the talking. He said, again, that she deserved much more; and repeated, too, that he was using up her life.

Then, for the forty minutes that were theirs, they spoke of love: as it had been for them, as it still was, of its confinement, necessarily so, its intensity too, its pain, the mockery it had so often felt like, how they had never wasted it by sitting in silence in the dark of a cinema, or sleeping through the handful of nights they'd spent together in her flat. They had not wasted it in lovers' quarrels, or lovers' argument. They did not waste it now, in what they said.

'Why?' she murmured when their drinks were almost finished, when the Running Footman was noisier than it had been, other office workers happy that their day was done. 'Please.'

He did not answer, then dragged the words out. It was in people's eyes, he said. In Chiltern Street it was what the bagwoman he gave alms to saw, and the taxi-driver in the Japanese café, and their waitress there, and the sleepy attendants of the picture gallery, and people who glanced at them in the Gardens. In all the places of their love affair – here too – it was what people saw. She was his bit on the side.

'I can't bear it that they think that.'

'It doesn't matter what people think. Come to the flat now.'

He shook his head. She'd known he would: impulses had never been possible. It was nothing, what he was saying; of course it didn't matter. She said so again, a surge of relief gathering. More than anything, more than ever before in all the time they'd been in love, she wanted to be with him, to watch him getting his ticket for the tube, to walk with him past the murky King and Queen public house at the corner of India Street, the betting shop, the launderette. Four times he'd been to the flat: two-day cases, in Liverpool or Norwich. She'd never wanted to know what he said in Dollis Hill.

'I don't mind in the least,' she said, 'what people think. Really I don't.' She smiled, her hand on his arm across the table, her fingers pressing. 'Of course not.'

He looked away and she, too, found herself staring at the brightly lit bottles behind the bar. 'My God, I do,' he whispered. 'My God, I mind.'

'And also, you know, it isn't true.'

'You're everything to me. Everything in the world.'

'Telephone,' she said, her voice low, too, the relief she'd felt draining away already. 'Things can come up suddenly.' It had always been he who had made the suggestion about his visiting her flat, and always weeks before the night he had in mind. 'No, no,' she said. 'No, no. I'm sorry.'

She had never asked, she did not know, why it was he would not leave his marriage. His reason, she had supposed, was all the reasons there usually were. They would not walk this evening by the murky public house, or call in at the off-licence for wine. She would not see him differently in her flat, at home there and yet not quite. It was extraordinary that so much should end because of something slight. She wondered what it would feel like, waking up in the night, not knowing immediately what the dread she'd woken to was, searching her sudden consciousness and finding there the empty truth and futile desperation.

'It's no more than an expression,' she said.

*

He knew she understood, in spite of all her protestations; as he had when when she arranged her divorce. It had become an agitation for her, being married to someone else, but he had never minded that she was. A marriage that had died, and being haunted by how people considered the person you loved, were far from the heart of love itself; yet these had nagged. They would grow old together while never being together, lines ravaging her features, eyes dulled by expectation's teasing. They would look back from their rare meetings as the years closed over this winning time and take solace from it. Was that there, too, in the bagwoman's eyes, and idly passing through strangers' half-interested reflections?

'I haven't explained this well,' he said, and heard her say there was tomorrow. He shook his head. No, not tomorrow, he said.

*

For longer than just today she had been ready for that because of course you had to be. Since the beginning she had been ready for it, and since the beginning she had been resolute that she would not attempt to claw back fragments from the debris. He was wrong: he had explained it well.

She listened while again he said he loved her, and watched while he reached out for the briefcase she had so often wanted to replace and yet could not. She smiled a little, standing up to go.

*

Outside, drinkers had congregated on the pavement, catching the last of the sun. They walked through them, her coat over his arm, picked up from where she'd draped it on the back of her chair. He held it for her, and waited while she buttoned it and casually tied the belt.

In the plate-glass of a department-store window their reflection was arrested while they embraced. They did not see that image recording for an instant a stylishness they would not have claimed as theirs, or guessed that, in their love affair, they had possessed. Unspoken, understood, their rules of love had not been broken in the distress of ending what was not ended and never would be. Nothing of love had been destroyed today: they took that with them as they drew apart and walked away from one another, unaware that the future was less bleak than now it seemed, that in it there still would be the delicacy of their reticence, and they themselves as love had made them for a while.